TOPLIN

Also Available by Michael McDowell

The Amulet
Cold Moon Over Babylon
Gilded Needles
The Elementals
Katie
Wicked Stepmother (with Dennis Schuetz)*
Blood Rubies (with Dennis Schuetz)*

* Forthcoming.

TOPLIN

A Novel by
MICHAEL McDOWELL

Illustrated by Harry O. Morris

VALANCOURT BOOKS

Dedication: For A.

Toplin by Michael McDowell
Originally published by Scream/Press, Santa Cruz, Calif., 1985
Reprinted by Dell Abyss in 1991
First Valancourt Books edition 2016

Text copyright © 1985 by Michael McDowell and Charles Santino
Illustrations copyright © 1985 by Harry O. Morris

Published by Valancourt Books, Richmond, Virginia
http://www.valancourtbooks.com

All rights reserved. In accordance with the U.S. Copyright Act of 1976, the copying, scanning, uploading, and/or electronic sharing of any part of this book without the permission of the publisher constitutes unlawful piracy and theft of the author's intellectual property. If you would like to use material from the book (other than for review purposes), prior written permission must be obtained by contacting the publisher.

All Valancourt Books publications are printed on acid free paper that meets all ANSI standards for archival quality paper.

ISBN 978-1-943910-18-2
Also available as an electronic book.

Cover illustration by Harry O. Morris
Set in Dante MT

Errors disappear like magic.
>   —Carton

This work is based on characters and basic story devised by Charles Santino. It could not and would not have been written without him.

MMM

She was, quite simply, the most hideous human being I had ever seen.

I

The grocery store was closed.

I hadn't expected that. I had passed that grocery store every day for I couldn't remember how many years, and it had never been shut at this hour. I had passed it every day on my way to work, and every morning it was open. It was open every evening on my way home from work. I never shopped there. I didn't like the looks of the place. But that evening in May, I needed a particular spice, and that store—I was unutterably convinced—carried it.

A sign on the door read:

> DEATH IN THE FAMILY
> BUT COME BACK SOON

I didn't believe it. There was something about the wording, something about the lettering that led me to believe that the shop was closed for some other, and very likely more sinister, reason. I couldn't help but feel that it was closed because of me. After all, I had passed it dozens, hundreds, thousands of times, and never wanted to go in before. That particular day in that particular year I wanted to go in, and it was shut.

Not only was I certain that the placard was meant especially and entirely for me, I knew that behind it was a condescending, derisive laugh. *Figure it out* the sign said with a shrug of its painted shoulders. *Determine why.*

I peered through the window. I remembered the owner, in his black pants and his white apron. I had glimpsed him through the window before. I peered through the glass. I had the feeling he was hiding behind the counter. That he ducked behind the slicer when I peered through.

I could see nothing. The lights were off. The two narrow aisles were empty. The clock on the wall gave the incorrect time. I suspected the owner, in an attempt to simulate a real closing, had unplugged his clock. I wasn't fooled. I knew that a funeral was an insufficient reason for holding back time. If there had been a real death in his family, he would have left the clock plugged in. Being greeted by the correct time on his return from the funeral would have provided consolation for the demise of his loved one.

I didn't trust the sign at all. I stared through the window for several minutes. The owner was fat and wheezing, and I knew he'd be uncomfortable crouching behind the meat counter. If I only waited long enough, he'd have to stand up and stretch his legs. I waited, but he was more patient than I. Or perhaps, I thought, he had a camp stool behind there.

Not wanting to be tested by a man who was obese and asthmatic, I decided that I wouldn't play his game. I walked off, inwardly vowing that from that day on, I'd take a different route to work and a different route home from work. He could keep his shop closed forever, on the same pretext, and I'd never know it. All his violent subterfuge would be wasted. I and my life would be unaffected by his crude stratagems.

There wasn't another grocery store between that one and home. I'd have to travel to another neighborhood to find my spice. Perhaps that was the object of the sign, I thought, to send me to another neighborhood. I wouldn't take the bait, I determined. I'd get along without the spice.

I couldn't get along without the spice. Recipes are followed exactly. I had had this recipe picked out for a long time. I wasn't going to give it up, and I wasn't going to do it half-heartedly. I walked on toward home, though I was no longer certain that that was my destination.

Something in the neighborhood scented danger to me. It never had before, though on occasions, danger had been near and real enough. It's an old part of the city, seen better days as they say, wasn't likely to see better ones for some time to come, dilapidated brick and brownstone, old shopfronts, tenements burned-out or at best only run-down, with a population of old Europeans arrived in this country before their own nations turned Communist, still speaking the old languages, still looking as if they had awakened this morning in Krakow, and Prag, and Bucharest, and

Kiev. Uninterpretable signs are everywhere, and you rarely understand the curses with which you are cursed.

I smelled danger. I saw two cars in a chase down a side street that was littered with children. I saw a string of parking meters that had been torn apart for their nickels and dimes. A young man and a young woman turned smoothly away as I approached—that smoothness that spells illicit drugs. I saw a drunk lying in the street, employing the curb as a pillow, screaming imprecise imprecations at every vehicle that passed. As I went by a pharmacy, a woman ran out screaming "Go to Hell! Go to Hell!" She wore a stained green slicker, army surplus boots, white socks, and a shapeless hat. A Negro, well over six feet tall, ran out after her and caught her when she became wedged between the bumpers of two parked automobiles. When he lifted her up, she kicked at him and at two more men—pharmacists by their white smocks—who rushed out of the shop. One she caught in his testicles, and the other's wrists she bit savagely. "Give it back! Give it back!" they shouted at her, and as I went on toward home, no longer certain that that was my destination, they dragged her back into the store.

I was suddenly aware of a vagueness that had been troubling me for some time. It arched and peaked in that narrow avenue I trod, that avenue that stank so palpably of danger. I felt out of kilter. These were the streets I walked home along every day, without fail, without variation, without sensation. And now, on this particular day in May, I was suffused with the sense that everything was quite changed, that everything had been taken up into the sky and some verisimilitudinous copy had been set down in its place—and all for my benefit.

I decided I wouldn't go home.

I'd eat out.

I never eat out. I have an unlimited file of recipes and therefore no reason to eat out.

I decided to eat in the restaurant that is at the corner of my own block, across from a derelict little park where people gather to drink cheap wine and settle drug deals. It's so unhealthy that even the pigeons shun it.

I pass the Baltyk Kitchen twice a day, six days a week, on my way to work and on my way home after work. I'd never been inside, and I'd heard about it from a man who lived in my building. He moved out one night very suddenly, and when the landlord came to clean the place up for the next tenant, he found the lodger's mistress in the closet. She'd been dead for two weeks. The windows of the Baltyk Kitchen were small and covered with sun-faded cafe curtains that might originally have been red, or perhaps purple. With my eyes the way they are, it was difficult to know. I didn't know what it was like inside—except for the narrow glimpse I'd get in the summer when the outside door would be propped open.

It's only one room, square and not very large. There's a bar along one side, and booths along the other, under the faded cafe curtains. In between there's a white tile floor and half a dozen tables. On each table there's a plastic carnation in a plastic catsup bottle.

It was already night in that place, though outside the sun was not even within an hour of setting. It was always night in the Baltyk Kitchen, I supposed. The place was open twenty-four hours a day, but between two and three a.m., it didn't serve liquor, owing to some catch in the city alcohol licensing regulations. Regulars bought three beers just before two a.m. and nursed them until the bar opened again at three.

I went to the bar and sat down. I don't drink, I don't need to. There was no waitress, no bartender. I reached over and took a menu and opened it, but it was in a language I didn't understand. I laid the menu open in front of me and looked at the pictures on the wall. There were photographs of European film stars, none of whom I recognized. There was a portrait of the Pope, with a border of carnations painted on the outside of the glass in the frame. There were travel posters, in bleached Agfa-color, aggrandizing the Warsaw Pact nations.

No one occupied the booths or the tables in the center of the room.

On one side of the bar, to my left, sat a middle-aged woman, neatly and respectably dressed, reading a paperback book. The remains of a meal had been pushed to one side.

On the other side, to my right, sat three men—truck drivers or stevedores wandered away from their docks and wharves, I surmised—each with a bottle of beer before him. Two of them had their heads down on the bar and were snoring. The third tilted his bottle slowly toward the ceiling and allowed a stream of pale anemic beer to drain into his mouth. He looked very drunk and very tired.

I waited and looked at the menu, trying to make out cognates.

The third man finished off his beer and laid his head down on the bar. Smoothly, as he did so, the second man wearily lifted his head, looked about blearily, and tilted his bottle slowly toward the ceiling. A stream of pale anemic beer drained slowly into his mouth.

They were guardians of the place, I decided. Two slept while the third kept drowsy watch.

The respectable, middle-aged woman on my left slowly and deliberately placed her book down on the bar, wiping the marble surface clean with a napkin before she did so.

She crushed the napkin and dropped it in her coffee cup. She swivelled her head and looked around. Only I and the three guardians were to be seen, but perhaps she was looking for someone else altogether.

"My husband was attacked by four hundred men!" she screamed at me. "He's dead."

I didn't say anything. Whether she was telling the truth or not, there was nothing to say.

She picked up her book again and diligently searched for her place. When she had found it, she merely set the book down again. "That was a year ago!" she shrieked. "He's dead!"

Still I said nothing.

"If he wasn't dead," she screeched, "do you think I'd be spending my evenings in a dump like this?"

I would have said something to her, but at that moment, as if the middle-aged woman's rhetorical question had been her cue, the dingy curtains that hid the tiny kitchen at the back were parted, and the waitress came into the room.

Suddenly, with a blinding clarity, I understood where all that evening's surprises had tended. The sign on the grocery window, so obviously false and contrived; the violence I had witnessed in the streets on my way toward my home; the peculiar slant of the evening sun which had convinced me that, against all habit and inclination, I should eat in the Baltyk Kitchen—all these things had propelled me to this place, this very stool on which I sat uncomfortably perched, at this particular moment of that particular day in May, only so that I might witness that waitress pausing in the deceptively simple motion of pushing aside the grease-stained linen curtains that hid the kitchen of this grimy restaurant.

It was the right and proper beginning of everything that was to come after. An entirely new phase of my life began at that instant. I—that is to say, my life up to that moment—died. I—that is to say, my life beyond that moment—was born.

I see that now. I did not understand it then. *Then*, I felt something else, something quite different.

I felt trapped in that instant, in that first moment of seeing her framed there, her hands behind her grasping the hems of that curtain, her stance taut and suspicious as she glanced over the restaurant and as her eyes fell upon me and lingered.

All those mercurial changes in pattern that I had noted that evening on my unsuspecting journey home from work had been arranged for the sole purpose of driving me into the Baltyk Kitchen, where I had never been before, in order to see this woman, of whose presence so near me, of whose very existence, I had been totally unaware. I had fallen into a trap and, involuntarily, I glanced toward the door and plotted my escape.

In the lurch to the door, I told myself, I might overturn a table. If so, I would not hesitate, wondering if I should right it. I would simply flee the place.

I did not flee. Her gaze held me.

She was, quite simply, the most hideous human being I had ever seen.

The disfigurements of her birth were compounded with the ravages of disease. I saw them in her face. Her mouth was a running sore. Her bulging eyes were of different colors. Her ears were slabs of flesh pillaged from anonymous victims of accidents. Her nose was a bulging membrane filled with ancient purulence.

I dragged my eyes away from her face.

Beneath her uniform I sensed—I smelled—even greater deformities. Her uniform, stained to a filmy translucence by God knew what manner of excretions, showed the irregularities of her skin beneath.

I looked away, gasping for my breath.

One of the sleeping guardians to my right raised his head and began to laugh, drunkenly. He turned to his friend who was already awake and asked, insultingly, "Why did Jesus Christ of Nazareth never eat pussy?"

His friend shook his head.

The riddler punched the third guardian awake.

"Because," he shouted, "every time he touched one it healed!"

The three guardians laughed, and I turned desperately away from the waitress, who was filling a glass with water. I knew it would be for me. I turned up the collar of my jacket, and my head shrank inside it.

The respectable-looking woman put down her paperback book once more and shrieked at me: "Don't do that! You won't cut out the noise that way! Look at what I use!"

She jumped onto the stool nearer me. I wouldn't have thought her capable of such spryness. She lifted the bands of white hair at the sides of her head and revealed large gray earmuffs. Their fur was stained and matted. I saw the rusted steel band that circled her neck.

"It keeps out all the noise!" she shrieked. "I can't hear traffic! I can't hear what they say to me! Wear these!"

She ripped off the earmuffs and flung them at me.

I caught them and placed them on the bar beside the glass of water the waitress had brought. My hands twitched and trembled.

I looked into the waitress's eyes, willing their difference in color to be resolved. They remained obstinately different. I did not dare look anywhere but at her eyes.

The basilisk withdrew.

I stared down at the menu again and would not look up.

The respectable woman gathered up her earmuffs, and with her paperback book thrust high up underneath her arm, departed. I heard her shoes scraping grittily on the tiled floor. I was alone with the three drunken guardians and the gruesome waitress, staring at a menu I could not comprehend.

As I sat, staring at the menu, not daring to look up or turn around or even to run, I thought of her life. It was—it must be—insupportable. Such an appearance precluded any sort of natural intercourse with other human beings. A walking aberration this young woman, so horrible that pity withered before her.

I was awed by her. Her ugliness filled me with a sense of urgency I had not felt for a long while. A *degree* of urgency, it occurred to me as I turned it over in my mind, that I had *never* felt before.

She stood before me, not two meters away, but so steadfast was I in my resolution not to look at her that I began—in the safety of my refusal to see her again—to examine, detail by detail, her loathsomeness as it was burned into my brain. I would pick apart her physical horror. I began with the feature that had first captured my single attention—her eyes.

Perhaps one of her eyes was a glass eye, I considered. That would account for the difference in color. Yet how much of a difference was there, really, I wondered. My sense of color is dim and has been for some time. I don't see what others see; or at least I perceive that I don't. At that moment, I longed for my old visual acuity to return. I wanted, for no motive other than to look at her eyes, to be able to distinguish the palette of light as I had once been able to, as everyone around me was able to. To me, one eye appeared brownish-green, one eye appeared brownish-violet. A cheap oculist, I considered. He gave her a glass eye that didn't properly match her real eye that remained.

So certain was I of the validity of this hypothesis that I began to postulate in what sort of accident she had lost her eye. Was it an impalement, a searing, a disease, a self-inflicted wound? Had her eyeball soured, had it burst, had it been scooped out, had it simply ceased to exist one morning when she woke in her narrow bed?

I glanced up quickly. She was staring at me. I tried to look at nothing but her eyes. I wanted to test my hypothesis.

One eye *must* be glass.

Yet I never got so high as her eyes.

I was arrested by her open mouth, that amazing hole that ought to have had a bandage over it. I longed for the reality of a Christ Who might heal it. I stared at her teeth as I had wanted to stare at her eyes. They were sharp, discolored, and assorted in size.

Her tongue lolled forward, a red bleeding centipede, and she spoke to me.

"Forty-eight hours," she said to me, in a thick but unidentifiable European accent. She jerked her blistered thumb toward the three drunken guardians to my right. "Forty-eight hours they've been here. Drinking beer. Telling nasty stories."

My vision travelled upward.

The pupils of her unmatched eyes dilated together.

Neither was glass. Both were real, and all the waitress's deformity, I took by this sign, was genuine, her only birthright.

I staggered to the washroom, dropped to my knees, and poured the contents of my stomach into the toilet bowl.

As I rose slowly to my feet, I happened to glance into the mirror.

I was bleeding.

Blood seeped in finely articulated drops from the corners of my eyes.

I fixed myself steady before the mirror. Choking down one more surge of vomit, I stared at those black tears that slowly coursed down my face and dripped one by one, in an inexorable rhythm, onto the porcelain of the sink.

Here was proof that I had entered a higher state of consciousness. Here was the marker that showed I had climbed to a higher plane of my being.

How I longed then for the full complement of my vision! The tears looked to me only a dull red that had been seared black. I had but the faintest, dark impression of color in them. Did I pray, I had prayed for no boon other than to see my bloody tears incrimsoned.

I leaned into the mirror and watched as the tiny bloody globes welled, one by one, thick and glabrous, from my torn tear ducts, as regular as the carved figures appear out of the shuttered doors of a mechanical clock. And as I watched and as the stoppered sink began to fill with my salted bloody tears, I thought of that other time—nine years before—when my real life had begun.

2

After the death of my mother, my eldest brother, who did not get along with my father, ran off. We never discovered where he went, and gradually we ceased even to think of him. My second brother and I continued to live at home with my father, a stern silent man. It was expected that my brother and I should work to help defray domestic expenses, though I suspect that my father could have gotten us through without the meager extra income that my brother and I provided. My father believed that work built character, which it does.

For many years I was employed as an usher at a film theatre around the corner from us, but during my last year in school this shut down, owing to I knew not what. For some years my brother had had a job with the City Park Service, doing maintenance work during the winter and working at the City Beach during the summer. He was able to secure me a position as a "Vendor" at the City Beach. I put "Vendor" in quotes because it was more than a generic description of my job. "Vendor" indicated a very precise slice of employment and was by no means the lowest position I could have been handed.

I might for instance have been a "Fry Cook," but I had no experience in that line. I could have been appointed a "Cashier," but this was employment given to girls. By far the greatest number of young men awarded summer jobs were merely "Groundsmen," but I had had my brother's recommendation, and perhaps his superior, for some reason unknown and unknowable to me, wanted to please my brother.

It would be my duty, at the smallest of the four City Beaches, to service the candy and soda machines, retrieving the accumulated coins and refilling them when necessary. On slow days, I was told, this would be no work at all. On busy days, I was given to understand, I would be run ragged.

My uniform would be black pants, white shirt, black shoes, black socks, and black-shaded sunglasses. Such an outfit as this on the beach would immediately mark me as an employee of the Service, and I might be required to give directions or answer simple questions about Park Service rules and facilities available to the public.

The city has several beaches, and I as a beginner was assigned to the beach farthest out and hardest to get to, with fewest facilities, and least frequently attended. It was at the narrow extremity of a strange curve of land that spiralled out into the ocean. The mainland at this point was a fairly substantial area of salt marsh, still quite wild and unbuilt up; the City jealously protected this area, the single wildlife refuge within its precincts. There was a fair-sized parking lot on the mainland, but access to the beach was only by foot, across a narrow boardwalk, nearly half a mile in length, that traversed the salt marsh. The sole employment of one of the Groundsmen was to patrol this boardwalk and to replace any single board that appeared rotten or looked about to split. The boardwalk was perfectly straight for its entire length, but it swelled into an arched bridge over the narrow tidal river that flowed through the salt marsh—toward the sea at low tide and away from the sea at high. Some boys found this bridge and the salt river that flowed swiftly beneath it to be of greater interest than the sea itself. There was always a bevy of teenagers huddled right at the peak of the arch, pushing one another off the bridge into the briny water below.

My brother, who was employed at another beach entirely, left me off in the parking lot every morning just after dawn, and I walked across the boardwalk to the beach. Occasionally I'd see, far ahead of me or far behind me, another solitary worker on his way to the concession stand, but just as often I'd find myself the sole traveller along the entire length of the boardwalk. My footsteps alone echoed there. Although I trod those planks but twice a day, I grew to know them well. They had both an auditory and a visual rhythm, became relatively dark and sonorous in one stretch and faded into a relative lightness and quietude in another. The salt marsh itself altered daily, according to the weather, according to the tides, according to some rhythm so subtle only the salt marsh itself could feel it and respond appropriately. Some days when I'd peer over the side of the boardwalk, the marsh would seem brown and limp and dead, with patches of cracked mud showing beneath the stiff grass. At other times, all would seem the freshest springlike green, bubbling and alive. From the boardwalk, one couldn't even see the high buildings of the city; they were hidden behind the dunes on the beach. The sky was an inverted blue cup tipped over the boardwalk and me.

On the far side of the boardwalk was a long, narrow strip of concrete with toilets and changing rooms in the center, and a concession stand at either end. My work took me back and forth along that strip of concrete, all day long. I had nearly two dozen keys on a long chain attached to my belt. That chain completed my costume of black trousers, white shirt, black shoes, black socks, and sunglasses. The chain was so heavy on my right side that I discovered my spine was compensating for it, and in the evening when I had taken it off, I listed heavily to the left. Thereafter I alternated the burden of metal keys, left to right, and back, precisely.

First thing in the morning, I went into the little windowless concrete room that was my office and checked to make certain that it and my cash boxes had not been broken into. Since most of the money was taken away by a park official every evening for counting and deposit, this would have been a greater nuisance than an actual loss, but it would have been, for me at any rate, a *considerable* nuisance. Then I went about and checked each of the vending machines, filling each to the limit of its capacity, spilling in a few coins to allow for change-making. After I had helped the cashier in each concession stand set up for the day—I being responsible for their cash boxes—a few hours were mine.

Despite the heat, I hid myself away in my little windowless office. It was these few hours of the day I hated the most, not because they were empty and I was without employ, but because of what was happening outside. It was at this time that bathers from the city began to arrive at the beach. In screaming hordes they trampled across the boardwalk, swarmed around the concession stands, filled up the toilets and changing rooms, and then flooded out over the dunes to the beach itself. Once, on a very hot Saturday morning at the very beginning of my tenure as a Vendor, I made the mistake of going over the breast of dunes to the sea myself.

The sea was a spread sheet of aquamarine studded with green diamonds, hemmed in white foam, cold and powerful and limitless. The narrow beach was a Purgatory of naked, burning, writhing, red, screaming, Hell-damned souls.

I didn't go back to the beach. I never crossed the breast of dunes again—except once.

When I was not engaged in the execution of a duty required by my position, I sat in my windowless concrete room, ovened by the sun. As I rolled coins, I brooded on the particolored Hell of humanity seething between me and the cold aquamarine sea.

I checked the vending machines again late in the morning and filled them to the brim for the lunch crowd. I filled them again shortly after lunch and emptied them of change late in the afternoon. I counted the cashier's receipts and, adding them to my own, prepared the collection bag for the day. As I had been very nearly the first to arrive each morning, so I was one of the very last to leave in the evening. My brother, nearly always, was waiting for me in the parking lot.

I have always wondered why men and women go on so about their jobs: how they're overworked, or even underworked, underpaid, how their positions are unsuited to their talents, how they are vilified by their coworkers, unappreciated by their employers, how their office hasn't any window, or how their lunch break comes at an inconvenient time. A job is a job. It never occurred to me to wonder if I were happy in mine or not. I did not imagine ways it could be made better, either on the point of efficiency, pay, or satisfaction to myself. I did what I was told, no more, no less, and without ever considering that the situation might in any way be improved.

This was perhaps a mistake.

Not on my part, certainly, for I was, in this passive manner, quite content. But my attitude evidently caused some rancor among the other employees. It soon became quite clear to me that I was not liked. And, because I had no interest whatever in what opinion the Cashiers, Fry Cooks, and Groundsmen held of me, their feelings must have been pronounced if I felt them at all. I'm not certain what they objected to, precisely. But I've found that people in general are a fuzzy-thinking lot, and they may not have known precisely either. I know for a fact, however, that I was resented because of my position. I had the senior spot at the beach, in the absence of any representative of the Park Service downtown; and as these men showed up only about twice a day, I was in charge most of the time. The only telephone, for instance, was located in my office; and once, when the father of one of the Cashiers died in the hospital, it was I who had to bring her the news. I was over them all, and yet I was also the least experienced. Every one of them, down to the lowliest Groundsman, had worked for the City Park Service for a longer time. This rankled them, I think, despite the obvious fact of my innate superiority. I knew, that is, that not one of them could have done the job as well as I, though I performed my duties without a twitch of effort.

And perhaps it was that, too, that displeased them. I don't recall that I flaunted my perfection, but I was much younger then and perhaps not so careful as I am now to conceal it. Perfection can bring a great deal of unnecessary and unwanted responsibility in this imperfect world. There may be other perfect men; on the other hand, I may be unique. But whatever the case, the world, if it knew me for what I really am, would seek to throw its burdens upon my shoulders. I prefer to fashion my own yoke, according to my personal taste. That is perhaps a selfish attitude, but selfishness in the perfect is not—cannot, by definition, be—a fault. I was efficient, and they were not. It may have come down to merely that. The Cashiers' trays never reconciled, the Fry Cooks boiled their thumbs, the Groundsmen were always having complaints preferred against them for rudeness. My portion of the business, on the other hand, went without hitch, and I was commended nearly every day for my handling of the position.

It may have been that I did not consort with them. I did not flirt with the Cashiers. I did not trade filthy stories with the Fry Cooks. And when I heard that two of the Groundsmen had been discovered with their pants down in the hollow between two dunes, I did not hesitate to turn them in—though they were otherwise, admittedly, our best workers. The other employees felt, in short, that whereas by dint of tender age and inexperience I ought to have been one of them, I was actually on the opposing side of the City Park Service. In their simple minds, I was the enemy.

The busiest day of the summer was of course July the Fourth. It happened that year to fall upon a Saturday, so that it was—if that were possible—even more crowded than it would have been otherwise. I kept going all morning long filling the vending machines with sodas and candy and cleansing them of their coins. Humanity, in stultifying waves, surged over the dunes toward the beach: screaming, sweating, bearing furled umbrellas before them like lances, with baskets that seemed more likely to hold ammunition than provisions, hauling infants under their arms with an absence of tenderness that suggested that the children were to be no more than cannon fodder. I expected every moment to hear the noise of gunfire.

In the middle of the afternoon, when the heat was at its worst, having accumulated around the concrete since early in the morning, I had ten minutes or so of respite in my tiny office. The walls there were blistering. I could scarcely breathe. But I fled there as if it had been a cool, wet, autumn day inside. I was not looking for relief from the heat so much as relief from the crowds. They licked away my being with their idiot tongues.

I sat with my feet on the desk. The floor had been hot beneath my shoes. The telephone rang. A man, who identified himself as being on the Holiday Desk at City Park Headquarters, asked me to walk from the edge of the boardwalk, following the line of the winding salt marsh river, all the way down to the sea. There had been reports, the man said, of several young persons making love on a sand bar, their obscene orgiastic couplings but ill-shielded by the marsh weeds.

I asked if the Park Service would not prefer one or more of the Groundsmen to do this, but the man on the Holiday Desk said that I had the greater authority and that it was my responsibility.

I did not question him further but agreed to do as he said. Perhaps if I had not been so anxious to be away from the concession stands, the toilets, and the changing rooms, I would have wondered a little more at the request. As it was, however, I was more than willing to take the route—it led me well away from the concrete, the dunes, and the beach itself. The marsh river was part of the wildlife refuge and off-limits to the bathers. I anticipated no more than a solitary stroll from the boardwalk to the sea and back again. Any couples frolicking in that area would surely be gone by the time I got there. After all, it had taken considerable time for someone to spot them, to complain, for the complaint to be relayed downtown, and for the Holiday Desk to telephone me.

Of course I know now that there is no Holiday Desk at the City Park Service and that I would have discovered this if I had telephoned back for a confirmation of my instructions, on pretense of some tiny clarification. But I was so glad of the excuse to abandon the machines and the Cashiers' calls for more change, that I did not *want* those welcome instructions countermanded.

It was all a trick, staged by my jealous coworkers.

On the busiest day of the year, when I was most needed at the concession stands, when my absence would be greatest felt and most likely to obtain for me a reprimand for dereliction of duty, they were sending me out on a snipe hunt. It was some confederate who had called, of course.

Underneath the boardwalk, the marsh is wide. From the concession stands, the river appears a distant furling blue ribbon. But only a little farther on, the marsh narrows considerably and becomes little more than a bordering of the tidal river itself. The marsh river winds and winds, bordered on both sides by grassy banks, eroding dunes, and stretches of rocky beach. I had never been along it, for it is off-limits to all but the one or two Groundsmen who desultorily patrol it a few times in the course of the day. Following this meandering course, sometimes trudging through the damp marsh grass, sometimes painfully hobbling along the sharp-stoned stretches of beach, I was soon out of sight and hearing of the holiday crowds. Again, and quite refreshingly, I was as alone *here* as when I crossed the boardwalk at dawn. I followed the river, keeping a lookout—as was my duty—for the loving, impatient couples who had strayed beyond the bounds of both the public beach and public propriety. I saw no one, and this did not surprise me. I very easily could have returned to the concession stand and claimed my duty done. But I pursued, and watched the gulls and terns diving for shellfish in the tidal river.

After a time, I came within sight of the sea. Far over to my left was the city itself, dim in the haze of the hot afternoon. Nearer, but comfortingly distant, were the black seething patches of bathers. I could hear nothing but the waves breaking on the narrow shore ahead of me and the sea birds circling in the air overhead.

In pursuance of what I perceived my duty, I followed the tidal river all the way to the sea. As if for proof of my having completed the journey, I knelt at the edge of the surf and held out my arms to be splattered with foam. The day was beastly hot, and nowhere hotter than on this unpeopled stretch of blistering sand and sharp rock. I in my uniform was not dressed for such burning as poured down out of the sky. I felt stultified. My breath came with difficulty as I rose to my feet.

A tern dived at my head. I dropped to my knees, gasping.

A second bird flew at me, and just as he swooped up, scarcely missing my cheek, he evacuated his bowels. My neck was splattered with the mess; I could feel its liquid warmth seep beneath my collar.

Terns are smaller, lither, handsomer seabirds than gulls.

I had blundered into their nesting ground.

More terns, screeching, flew at me.

I shaded my eyes with one arm and folded the other arm over the top of my head. I staggered to my feet and shuddered along back toward the tidal river. The terns continued to dive at me.

The bill of one tern pierced the back of my wrist. I felt horrifyingly sharp pain and jerked my hand away. I felt the weight of the bird, temporarily caught by its beak in my flesh. It did a little staggering dance in the air, regained its aerial balance, and veered off.

Another bird attacked my unprotected head. I felt as if a pick had been dropped from a height onto my skull.

I struggled forward, waving my hand in front of me. I could see blood on it. I looked down at the ground, not daring to look up. A tern swooped down from above, up under my outstretched, protecting arm, and went for my eye. I jerked my head aside just

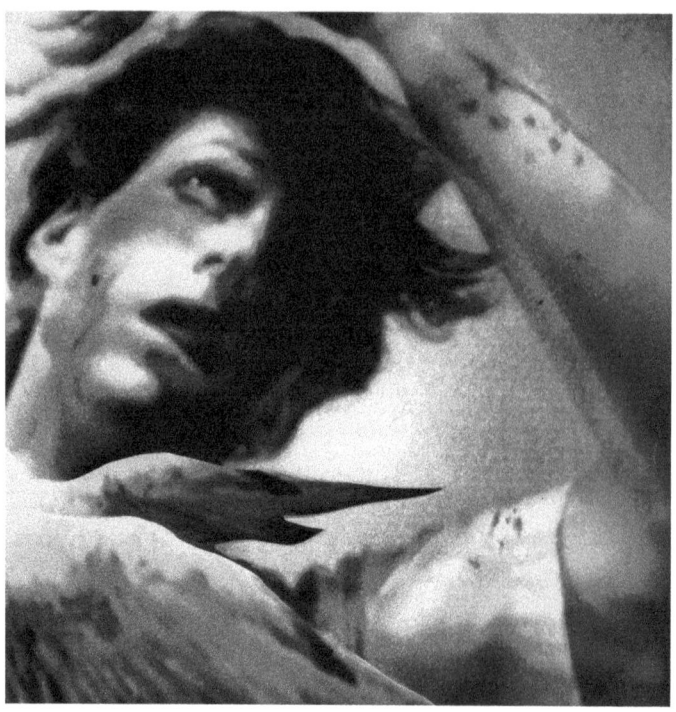

I struggled forward, waving my hand in front of me.

in time. It pierced my cheek. I could smell the bird's sun-dried stink. I could feel its beak opening and closing *inside* my mouth. I reached up, grabbed the bird by its legs—breaking one of them, I think—and pulled it out of my cheek. Its beak, at that moment, closed over the edge of my tongue, and as I pulled it out, it took away a little wedge-shaped morsel. I flung the bird aside and staggered onward.

I do not know how long I continued thus, but it was for some time. Only once did I look up, and then for but a fraction of a second. Here is what I saw: what must have been fifty or more terns, wheeling in a tight circle about twenty feet above me and about thirty feet ahead of me. They were anticipating my onward flight. But above them, in a much larger circle, flew the gulls, crying in their raucous stupid voices, voyeurs of the attack.

One of the terns dropped out the tight circle and dived at me.

My entire body jerked to one side, and the bird glanced shearing up my bare arm. I heard my skin rip like cellophane.

I stumbled on in the heat. I remember now quite precisely what I was thinking. Oddly, I did not think of how to save myself. Defense had become automatic. My body knew what it must do to protect itself; or at any rate, my mind could do no better. It seemed to me, as I stumbled forward, that the terns were mocking me—and that that mockery was their purpose even more than, say, defense of their nesting area. They mocked my helplessness, they mocked my stupidity and my sad, stumbling flight. Terns are shining white with at most a cap of black. They were, I knew, angry that I imitated their black-and-white plumage, but failed to reproduce the concomitant grace of their flight. To them I was an ugly, stupid thing; so ugly and so stupid that I deserved punishment for my innate shortcomings and ineptitude. My presence, in black and white, was an affront to their dignity and station.

Those were my first thoughts.

I fell into the water of the tidal river, spilling sideways. The brackish water entered my mouth, and the terns dived and pierced my side. I pulled myself up, spewing out the salty water from my mouth, and dragged myself on.

The shock of the water—for I had fallen into it unawares—changed the direction of my thoughts entirely. The terns were no longer birds in my mind. They were mankind itself, mankind at its worst, malicious and stupid. They knew—or ought to have known—that I had no designs upon their nests, their eggs, or their young. They attacked me because *attack* was a concept tattooed on the convolutions of their miniscule brains. And above them, in the larger, looser, noisier circle, the gulls displayed mankind at its best, passive and stupid. The gulls were unable to make sense of a situation whose parameters were patently obvious. I was surrounded by all humanity, and all humanity was either a tern or a gull. All stupid, and all either passive or dangerously malicious. And I, the perfect outcast, the faultless stranger, stumbled along through the salt water, pecked and bleeding and—in one final swoop of two terns in tandem—blinded.

I was hospitalized briefly.

Unable to see, I had groped along the edge of the river back toward the concession stands, where the afternoon exodus from the beach was starting up. Very probably I was an unwelcome, unwholesome sight to that burned pack of the damned.

A Groundsman led me back to my office. A Cashier took my head on her lap and wiped the blood from my scalp and my face, crying out in disgust at the wounds that were revealed underneath. A Fry Cook telephoned for the ambulance.

I was told that my eyes would heal properly. The birds' slicing beaks had scratched but not punctured the corneas. My head was bandaged for eight days.

When the bandages were removed and once the blurriness had subsided, my visual perception seemed to me as keen as before. That is, I still tested out at 40-20, able to see at a distance just about twice as well as normal. But there was one vast difference. I no longer saw colors as before. The intensity had faded dramatically. It was as if before I had dealt with a spectrum several meters wide, and now all the color range I had would fit onto a graph not more than a few centimeters in width. Everything —excepting blacks and whites—was only various shades of gray to me. The whole world looked washed-out, faded, as if every object, every plane, every vista had a hole in the bottom of it out of which the color had seeped for a long while, leaving only a suggestion of the brilliance and variety of former hues. I could distinguish red and blue and yellow, though sometimes only with concentration—but for me, magenta, heliotrope, viridian, vermillion, cobalt, umbre, ochre, sienna, crimson, and canary—all these subtle differentiations of the palette were lost.

The Park Service was obligated to pay for my hospital bills, and those coworkers involved in the practical joke were discharged, but still I did not return to my job at the beach. I began, in those weeks of my recuperation, to ignore the tiny range of color that was left to me, and I concentrated on what I still could see—the whites and blacks. And in those antipodes I discovered almost infinite variation. It was for this reason that I maintained the black and white Park Service uniform as my normal dress and have retained it, with some small changes, ever since. Older now, and with my Employer to mollify, I wear a suit. But still I have the black trousers, the black shoes, the white shirt, the black socks.

The wounds inflicted by the birds were, for the most part, superficial. I have a triangular incision in my tongue that produces a whistle whenever I talk rapidly—but I rarely talk at all. I have a small round scar, rather like a concave mole, where that tern pierced my cheek. And on my scalp are four small places where hair will not grow. I was told that the birds had actually pierced the skull and that beneath my scalp the bone is fractured like tiny spiders' webs.

I was perfectly well, but at the expense of the City Park Service, I recuperated for the remainder of the summer. My father died in August. For his funeral I purchased my first suit (S-1) and, in my brother's taxi on the way back from the crematorium, I began reading the Help Wanted advertisements in the newspaper. On the following day I was hired by my Employer, and the day after that I found the apartment where I live now. My brother offered to give me half the furniture that had belonged to my mother and father, but I declined. I had never liked my parents so much that I wished to be reminded of them every time I walked into a room.

I returned, now and then, to the hospital. I was advised to have plastic surgery to deal with the scars, but these, I maintained, were not noticeable. Such surgery would have been much more at my expense than for my profit. I never spoke of the diminution of my sense of color. That was a very private thing. It was, of course, the price I had paid.

I had traversed Purgatory. I had come as near Hell as any man might and live to tell of it. I was given knowledge and insight and was forever branded—by those four wounds on my scalp and the fifth wound in my cheek—as an outcast of humanity.

In exchange for my eyes' paltry ability to distinguish the narrow range of light we call color, I had gained nothing short of Vision Itself.

3

I flushed away my vomit, washed my face, and retied my tie, all the while inwardly screwing my courage to the sticking-place. A man who had suffered as I had suffered, to win such a prize as had been vouchsafed to me, was not the man to tremble before a woman, be she Basilisk or Gorgon or Medusa. When I left that tiny, evil-smelling washroom, I'd look the waitress in the face. My eyes would sweep down her body and seek out the farthest limit —the very frontier—of her repulsiveness.

I opened the door of the washroom cautiously and stepped out. I looked about. The first of the guardians—the one who had sat nearest me—was awake now, drowsily swilling a beer. My first renewed glimpse of the waitress was from the back. Beneath her uniform, her flesh roiled and seethed with contagion. I was revolted and staggered back to my place at the bar.

The waitress was placing a glass of water before a Negro who had just come in and seated himself at one of the tables between the bar and the booths. I turned and watched *him*, for I still could not bring myself to look at *her*. He was handsome in his way, with slicked-back hair and an oiled black beard. He wore black clothes and carried two large white shopping bags without logos. He had placed these at the side of the table and was rummaging in them. He had not seen the waitress. I waited for him to sit up straight and catch sight of her. I wanted to gauge his stupefaction and terror.

Infuriatingly, he remained immersed in his bags, peering into their depths, shoving about whatever was inside, blowing into them heartily.

When he finally pulled up, the waitress was already walking away. He had not seen her.

Despite my resolution in the washroom, I looked everywhere but where she was. She came and stood before me. My eyes drifted upward, and I saw a chalkboard, hung on a rope attached to a pulley. Every day, I supposed, it was lowered, and the daily special chalked on it. Then it was raised to a position of prominence above the bar.

I couldn't make out what the special was. It was written in the same incomprehensible language as the menu, but there was, fortunately for me, only one item on it.

Without looking at the waitress, I pointed to the chalkboard above the bar.

"The special," I said, with such weakness I had difficulty in recognizing my own voice. "I'll have the special."

She walked away toward the kitchen, and I lowered my eyes from the chalkboard with relief.

She called out in the incomprehensible language and there was a brief, responding chatter from the hidden purlieus of the kitchen.

The Negro called out an order for a beer.

The waitress—I could tell by the sounds she made in doing it—opened the cooler, took out a bottle, snapped off the top, and brought it around. I still did not look.

I turned and watched the Negro. Now surely he would see her.

Would he be crushed by the sheer weight of her distortion, I wondered. Would he vomit, as I had vomited?

In a crescented array on the table before him, the Negro had set out eight statues, in plaster, of a cartoon mouse and his cartoon mouse consort. Two pairs of the mice had been painted in what I supposed were vibrant colors. The other two pairs remained unpainted—pale, livid plaster figures, with chalky grins.

He looked up at the waitress. "Which one for the beer?" he asked, with the same chalky grin as the mice.

He stifled his repulsion so effectively that I, attending closely, did not see it at all. It was as if, for this man protected by his crescent of plaster mice, the waitress were a perfectly normal young woman, in a soiled white uniform, bringing him a bottle of beer.

"No," she said. "No trade. No money, then get out."

"Take two," he urged. "Take a pair. Sweet, for your kids." I was horrified on three counts. It seemed a gross insult for the Negro to hint that she might be a mother; the utter impossibility of it only called attention to the depth of her deformity. And in a deeper way I was horrified to postulate the existence of any child so star-crossed he must call her mommy. And, thirdly, what moral, aesthetic criminal could couple with such as she, so as to produce so unfortunate a child? No sane man.

"No," said the waitress. "Out."

"Painted. Plain," said the Negro, pointing at his statues. "One painted, one plain."

The waitress put down the bottle of beer out of the Negro's reach. She picked up two of the statues and thrust them down into one of the shopping bags.

The Negro protested, and with a wide sweep of his arms, as if he were a black Niobe protecting the last of her grinning children, he gathered the mice against his breast.

The plaster mice grated and cracked and split apart in his embrace.

The Negro stood up in a wail of anguish. The plaster mice slipped and slid onto the floor, and collapsed in clouds of white powder. Fragments of grins and hands and button shoes remained of the painted figures, held together only by the paint.

"Nobody come near!" he screeched, and with the only remaining whole figure—one that had fallen outside his embrace—he fled to a position of defense between the unplugged juke box and the wall.

"Look at this mess!" cried the waitress, in just such a tone of exaggeration as any normal young woman in soiled uniform, whose duty it was to keep the place clean, might have spoken.

"Trash!" she cried, picking up the two shopping bags and tossing them out the door.

The Negro, running toward the door, screamed, "I've been robbed! I've been robbed!"

He tripped in the plaster dust and fell against one of the tables. It overturned, and he slipped along its smooth surface to the floor. The last of his plaster figures was crushed beneath him. In his frustration, he began kicking violently against other tables, overturning them. He pushed over chairs, spilled carnations and water and catsup bottles, salt shakers and little dishes filled with packages of sugar.

The first of the guardians—the one who was awake during this—slowly slid off his stool and staggered over to the Negro. He reached down with his arms outstretched, caught the black man under his arms, and lifted him to his feet. The Negro's feet shuffled comically in the plaster dust and painted grins of his smashed statues. One too-large shoe slipped off his foot. The buttons of his shirt popped and flew. His pants began to slip off his hips, and he made more comical attempts to hold them up.

The guardian suddenly let the Negro drop onto the floor again.

All the change then poured out of the Negro's pockets and settled in the plaster dust or spun beneath the overturned furniture. I followed the progress of one particular quarter as it rolled purposefully toward the waitress and came to rest between her feet. I looked away again.

"Throw him out," said the waitress to the guardian.

"My money!" cried the Negro.

"That is for damages," said the waitress and stood aside as the guardian lifted the Negro once more, pushed him toward the door, and propelled him out onto the sidewalk.

The sun had set behind the tall buildings in the west of the city. Evening was falling over my neighborhood. It was a mockery of normalcy.

Two old European women in shapeless flowered dresses came out of the kitchen, surveyed the wreckage without surprise or anger, and set about righting things, with the air of *We've done this before.*

"Police!" the Negro shouted just outside the door. "Police! I've been robbed!"

The waitress began picking up the Negro's change and putting it into the pocket of her dress.

Unperturbed, the guardian came back to his bar and his beer.

The Negro continued to shout for the police. The police did not come. In the scuffle, he had lost both his shirt and his right shoe. The waitress picked them up and dropped them behind the juke box.

When the place was very nearly set to rights again, the Negro came stealthily back inside the restaurant. He sat in the booth nearest the door.

I and the waitress and the guardian who was awake looked at him.

"I've got a gun," said the Negro. "I'm going home and get it and come back and shoot your husband."

The Negro evidently thought that the waitress was married to the guardian who had thrown him out.

"My husband in Novgorad," said the waitress, still gathering up change.

The Negro, as if he had forgotten that this money was part of his grievance, took no notice of her action.

"I'm a lawyer," said the Negro. "And I'm going to sue you and your husband for every penny you've got."

This made no impression. The waitress came nearer me. There were nickels around the base of the stool on which I was seated. I was nauseous with the thought that she might inadvertently brush against the leg of my trousers. I would burn the entire suit if she did. (Though it was Suit S-4, my favorite, I did not hesitate to make such a resolution.) I would spend the night in the bathtub. I might shave the hair from my legs.

"I'm a doctor," said the Negro. "And I'm going to write you a prescription that's pure poison."

I moved around the corner of the bar, under pretense of looking at a newspaper that had been left there.

The waitress gathered up the change from around my bar stool. When she had moved away, I returned. I brought the paper with me, not because I had any interest in it, but to maintain the fiction that my movement away from the waitress had been casual and unpremeditated.

The Negro went through a long list of occupations and allied threats and finally concluded: "If you don't give me twenty dollars, I'm going to take back my statues."

All his statues were smashed.

"Where's your shoe?" demanded the waitress. She went over to the booth where he sat. "Where's your shirt?"

The two old women went back into the kitchen, where—I supposed—they resumed preparation of the special I had ordered, some time ago now.

"Get out!" said the waitress. "No shirt, no shoe. Get out!"

*

My dinner was brought me: a stringy, gelatinous stew, cooked with misshapen lumps of discolored potato. I wouldn't be able to eat any of it, I knew, if the waitress remained behind the counter where at any moment I might chance to look up and see her. She put down my plate and walked off.

I was relieved. I would be able to eat. It wasn't that I was hungry. I wasn't hungry at all. I had other things on my mind besides my stomach. But I didn't want to appear as if I were thinking of anything but the assuagement of my appetite. I wanted to seem normal, to the waitress and to the three guardians, two of whom were fast asleep again, still holding onto their empty bottles, snoring.

In my relief I looked up at her retreating figure. I must have looked up too quickly, for she turned to glance at me. I hadn't expected that. I hadn't counted on being made to suffer once more that terrible, uneven gaze.

I was hideously shocked—not by the difference in the color of those eyes, I was almost used to that now—but rather by the sudden realization that I had seen those eyes before, that particular gaze.

And what was worse, I remembered where.

I stiffly shook my head, signifying: *No sorry I don't want anything you can go away now and sit down.*

She did just that, seating herself at one of the tables behind me. If I didn't go to the trouble of turning around, I wouldn't see her. I could pretend she wasn't there at all and eat the stew she had brought me.

I lifted a spoonful to my mouth and tried not to remember that, with her hands, the waitress had touched the bowl, and the plate beneath the bowl, and the spoon I was lifting to my lips.

On the edge of the plate I noticed a bloody fingerprint—hers, the waitress'. Probably she had cut her finger while retrieving one of the Negro's coins from the welter of plaster shards on the floor. I lifted the bowl from the plate and discovered a pool of the waitress' blood, lurking beneath my stew. It boiled and sizzled.

As I carefully lowered the bowl of stew to hide that bubbling pool, I again remembered where I had seen that gaze before.

When my mother died, I was left alone with my father and

In a puff of oily smoke it rose up to the ceiling . . .

my two older brothers. My eldest brother fled, and what became of him my father and my second brother and I never found out. My second brother drove a taxi. My brother's taxi was involved in an accident with a city bus on a narrow street in this very neighborhood—out in front of this very restaurant if I remembered correctly. It was an unpleasant coincidence and savored of a malicious if not actually malevolent force of Fate in the Universe. The driver of the bus was killed. One passenger suffered a broken arm, the others—all Negroes—were unhurt. My brother's body was crushed in the impact. His face was lacerated with glass from the smashed windshield. I went to visit him in the hospital, and I saw, walking into his room, that he would never be presentable again.

My brother, carefully examining my expression, saw it too.

He died of his wounds, the doctor said.

My brother committed suicide. He willed himself not to live. He saw in my eyes that he would never be presentable again, and he gave up the ghost. His spirit was exhaled through his lips. I saw his parched, shredded lips open. A gust of fetid air that was my brother's soul puffed out of his mouth and rose up toward the ceiling.

My presence gave my brother the strength to die. The horror in my eyes, on seeing him, took away his hope of living but encouraged him to perish.

I stood at the foot of the bed, looking at him, disgusted but unable to look away. My brother spat out his soul between his parched, lacerated lips.

In a puff of oily smoke it rose up to the ceiling, hovered a moment in a corner, frustrated of egress. It left a stain, but the nurse and the doctor, when they came, did not notice it.

The ceilings of hospital rooms are stained with the oily residue of souls spat out of dying patients' parched mouths.

The waitress sat behind me. Now and then she shifted her weight and her chair scraped grittily on the tiled floor. I thought of her eyes, understanding why, despite their alien qualities, they were so familiar.

I don't speak of the difference in their color. I couldn't be entirely certain of that difference anyway. The diminution of my sense of color didn't allow me to gauge it.

In those marble eyes, those jewel-like eyes, I saw what I had seen once before, and unmistakably, in my brother's ruined face in the hospital. I saw the desire to be dead. Nothing more, and nothing less.

4

Like a mustard seed blown by mischance into the narrow crevice in a granite wall, the waitress of the Baltyk Kitchen took root in my life-hardened soul, weakening it, threatening to split it, spoiling its wholeness and symmetry. She was a foul blade rising from a grain buried the very moment I first saw her.

She was the latch, the spring, the key, to everything that came after. She blinded me with a harrowing Stygian light. Her halo was forged in hell.

She was a burnt puppet on a charred string, and I decided to follow her home.

Unmerciful to myself, I swallowed the stew, gagging bite by gagging bite. At the end I lifted the bowl. Her blood still boiled on the plate beneath.

I pushed away the plate and the bowl and ordered coffee and strudel. I bowed my head and became the fourth guardian at the bar, but without the benumbing benefit of alcohol. When she brought the plate with the strudel, she left a bloody thumbprint on the rim. Her blistered thumb had been wrapped with a paper napkin, but that improvised and inadequate bandage was now soaked through with blood. I pushed away the strudel untasted and drew back as she brought my coffee.

She left a thumbprint on the saucer. I carefully lifted the cup and pushed the saucer away.

I drank slowly, holding my hand over the cup to prevent a too rapid cooling. I did not know how long I would have to wait before she went home. I tried without success to imagine her on the street, presenting her Medusa-face and Medusa-form to the most casual passerby.

Other customers came in and took places in the booths and looked at the menus and placed their orders and did not object when the dishes with the bloody thumbprints were placed before them.

I sat and drank my coffee and laid the plans for my great project.

I would help this young woman. I would wring my heart and sprinkle the pity of my heart's blood on her parched life. I would validate my own perfection, and at the same time I would ease her out of her trudging misery.

I would help her die.

That death was her only, her constant thought was obvious to me. It was in every gesture of her quivering limbs. It was in the light of the gaze of her mismatched eyes. Death was a song in her distended throat.

For her poor, piteous, mangled sake, I would see to it that she died, and died soon.

For my own sake, I would see that she died, and died as quickly as I could bring the deed about in a manner commensurate with the advancing of my spirit and—contrariwise—the eclipsing of her own blighted soul.

It was night out now, in my neighborhood. Inside the Baltyk Kitchen, the harsh fluorescent lights embedded in the tin ceiling had been switched on with a flick of her bloody thumb.

One of the old women in the kitchen came out and called her by name: Marta.

When Marta was dead, the world, unquestionably, would be a more beautiful place.

I looked forward to the passage of years. Sometime, I said to myself, I would be able to walk by this place and think inconsequentially "Ah yes, this is the restaurant where Marta worked. Marta's expiring breath blessed my compassion." And the memory would be no more terrible than the knowledge that at this same corner but in the street, my brother's taxi was struck by a bus full of Negroes and Negresses.

Yet every time I allowed myself to be comforted by such a projection, I'd look up and there I'd see Marta herself.

I had, in short, my work still to do.

It would be my finest hour.

Her shift ended at nine o'clock. So much I overheard her say to the third guardian, the one who was awake at the moment. Yet as he had not asked her anything of the sort and in fact had not spoken a word to her all evening long, I suspected that the information was meant for me.

Half an hour remained.

I went into the washroom and locked the door. It stank of my vomit, alien and unpleasant to me now.

I closed the lid of the toilet, placed my kit atop it, and in my usual fashion of holding one end of the zipper with the thumb and middle finger of my left hand, unzipped it with the thumb and second finger of my right.

I took out my scissors and cut off two small hairs that

protruded from my nostrils. With clippers I snipped off an unevenness on the smallest fingernail of my right hand. I rubbed my lips with a finger of Vaseline. With tweezers I ripped a hair that I discovered growing on the curl of my ear.

A man beat on the door to get in, but I said, "Go away!"

I looked into the mirror and contemplated my reversed image with intense satisfaction. I remained in the washroom twenty-three minutes. My stool augured success. The condition of my stool is as infallible a prognostication as the endless, coiling bowels Manto ripped from the bleeding belly of the sacrificial calf and described for her blind father.

When I came out again, Marta's replacement had already arrived. Marta was not to be seen. I was panicked. All my resolutions were predicated on action taken *tonight*. I would not, could not return and begin all anew. Tonight, not any other night, I would follow Marta home and discover where she lived. I nervously paid my check and counted my change three times, glancing agitatedly all about me and particularly at the clock, hoping that Marta had not already left.

The clock read eight-fifty-nine. The second hand surged up toward the Roman numeral XII. At exactly nine o'clock, Marta pushed aside the curtains into the kitchen. She had not changed out of her uniform but had merely added to it a black-and-white checked scarf.

I stood very still and looked away, as if I were figuring out how much to leave as a tip. I left too much.

I did not need to look at Marta. Her presence was too strong for me not to be cognizant of her every movement behind me. She went toward the door.

"Marta!" cried the second waitress, who had taken her place. "This is for you."

The waitress had gathered up the coins I had left and held them out in her cupped hands.

Marta came back to the bar.

I was paralyzed. I couldn't move, I couldn't even look away. Hell and Damnation itself might have stalked across the floor toward me, oozing pain and dribbling agony with every suppurating step, and I would not have been half so shaken.

She shone in the night, pale and sickly, a beacon on that ill-lighted street.

Marta took the coins in her own cupped hands and said, "Thank you, sir."

She spilled the coins into the pocket of her dress and went out.

I wiped my brow and followed.

I trailed her at a distance of some meters. It was night, the neighborhood was dark. The globes of the streetlamps had been broken long ago and repaired only along the principal thoroughfares. She took me along a side street. I watched *her*, not where she was leading me. I dropped back a few more meters in case she should turn. I had no difficulty in following her. She shone in the night, pale and sickly, a beacon on that ill-lighted street.

She paused at the corner. I took the opportunity to look about.

We were on *my* street. I was standing before the stoop of *my* apartment building.

I bit my lip until I could taste the blood.

Every night, I must then suppose, she walked by my own apartment building, while I was inside, preparing the day's particular recipe. I involuntarily glanced upward. There were my windows, one, two, three floors above the ground. I might have glanced out any one of those three windows any particular evening and seen *her*, glowing, shambling along the sidewalk.

With shame I contemplated my own former ignorance and innocence.

How could I, all these years, have thought to maintain the framework of my existence when she passed ritualistically beneath my windows twice each day?

She crossed the avenue there. Trembling with anger, I followed.

I lessened the distance between us. If she heard me, she did not turn. She did not hurry her pace. A woman like that, I surmised, need not fear rape.

Ahead, in the darkness of the street not lighted by her phosphorescence, I became aware of a sound, a compound noise of breath and small animals and shuffling feet and squeaking wooden wheels.

Marta stopped. I stopped and ducked behind an elevated stoop.

The compound noise left off, its components winding down variously.

"Good evening," said Marta.

"Hey how you," said a voice in return.

Behind the stoop I heard Marta's steps again. Then the shuffling, the squeaking wooden wheels, the animals' breath. I jerked out from behind the stoop and followed after Marta.

I met, on the sidewalk, a Negro, about sixty, down-trodden by life but not derelict. He was drawing behind him, on a stout white cord, a toy train: locomotive, three hopper cars, and caboose, each of wood and about a foot long. To each of the hopper cars, by a length of colored string, was tied a fat beribboned cat that progressed steadily with the train and looked to neither side, but moved with staid resolution. Nestled inside each of the three main hopper cars was another beribboned cat, these, however, being more curious, with their heads moving slowly from one side to another. A single kitten was strapped—cruelly it seemed to me—to the top of the caboose.

"Hey how you," said the Negro to me as I passed him.

I nodded but did not speak.

Ahead of me, Marta went up a stoop. I marked it well. I sneaked closer. I was near enough to hear her fumble with keys. I sank flat against the wall of her building. I heard the outer door open. Dimly then I heard the scrape of the inner door. Marta was inside.

I counted three, then peeled away from the building. I came around to the foot of the stoop. There were her prints, glowing, up the stairs. A deeper, shimmering puddle right in front of the door showed where she had paused with the keys.

I stood looking at her building with as much horror as, several hours before, I had first seen Marta herself. The brutal significance of her address pounded me into the earth.

It was not that she lived on the same street as I—that I could have taken as merest coincidence. Five thousand men, women, and children live on that street. Similar ironic or bizarre situations arise all the time in cities of a certain density of population. Just because I found myself at the center of one of those statistical improbabilities was no reason for me to feel threatened. No, it wasn't because she lived on my street that I was disturbed, it was for another reason.

The Baltyk Kitchen was located at the beginning of our street, where the numbering commenced. It bore a large ONE painted on the glass above the doorway. Marta lived at number NINETY-FOUR.

And I, I reflected bitterly, lived at number FORTY-SEVEN, exactly halfway between. That was more than coincidence. That was perfidy and plotting.

On her way to the restaurant during the day, she would no doubt pause before my building and say to herself, *I'm halfway there.*

And tonight, in following her away from the restaurant, I had noticed a hitch in her gait as she passed my building again. *I'm halfway home*, that said, and nothing else.

It was as if my entire life were nothing but a milestone, a

halfway marker for Marta. I felt used. I was sickened in the very well-springs of my existence.

Events were moving rapidly forward.

5

I was walking away, walking home thoughtfully, through the dark night of my neighborhood. It wasn't the same for me any longer. It was all changed. The similarities I noted in the buildings, in the streets, in the array of broken street lamps and bent and twisted signposts were only a mockery of verisimilitude. I hadn't realized until that moment with what deep affection I had regarded that neighborhood. Now it was all spoiled, of course, by my knowledge of Marta's existence.

But would Marta's departure restore the neighborhood to its former condition? I wasn't certain, but I still saw no other way to proceed.

It was in just such a reverie, thinking just such thoughts, that I proceeded down my quiet dark street, passing one by one in descending order the numbers from NINETY-FOUR toward FORTY-SEVEN, when quite suddenly I was jolted from behind. Upset. Nearly knocked to the pavement. I tripped and spun giddily in hope of maintaining my balance. And I heard laughter, women's laughter. I lurched, swayed, and pressed myself upright against a lamppost. I could feel the sharp blistering paint through the sleeve of my suit jacket. (S-4 is worn thin toward the elbows.) I stared ahead of me.

There were two women bustling along. It was they who had knocked into me. The insulting timbre of their laughter told me the collision had been deliberate. They looked back over their shoulders. I was momentarily able to make out their faces in the light from a lamp shining out of a ground-floor apartment window.

Their faces were identical, identically featured, unmirrored images of each other. Their laughter, cadenced and musical, might have been a tape recording, played at once on two machines.

Yet though dressed alike, in black trousers, white blouses, and black jackets, they were readily distinguishable. The hair of one had been bleached a shining white; the hair of the other had been dyed a jetty black.

They turned their heads and hurried on. Their jackets bore insignia—an hour glass with wings. And beneath the hourglass, ticked out in chrome studs, the legend TEMPUS FUGIT.

The two women—they must have been twins—hurried on and disappeared around a corner. I continued straight on toward home. I reached my own stoop and paused. I looked up at my own darkened windows. I decided not to go in, after all. I was too keyed up, too full of my project. It seemed to me that I had been, before Marta, a mere automaton of a man, without purpose and without drive.

Now I had a mission, a reason for even the smallest motions of my existence. Everything I did from this moment on, every raising of my foot, every lowering of my fingers upon a table, would be fraught with significance.

I could retrace my steps to Number NINETY-FOUR and investigate which apartment was Marta's. I knew she lived alone. Who could rest, knowing of her presence in an adjoining room? Or I could go on, past my own building, back toward the Baltyk Kitchen.

This I did. I gave the appearance of a man strolling in the evening, a casual post-prandial peregrination. And in fact, it was casual, for I had no motive in mind other than the cooling of my fevered brain.

There were only a few persons out at that hour: old men who had no homes at all, old women whose lazy daughters had sent them out on some paltry errand, old children who had already learned too much of the world and the world's way. All moved quickly and surreptitiously and silently along the street, sidling shadow to shadow, eyeing me and one another with undisguised mistrust.

I was within a number or two of the Baltyk Kitchen when I heard voices, low, growling, drunken, and I recognized the three guardians. They stood in a shadowed recess just this side of the restaurant, pissing in unison against a wall of rough masonry.

They had transferred their ordering intact: the first guardian still stood left-most, the third guardian was still on the right.

"A hundred lovers . . ." said the first.

"A *million* lovers," corrected the second, energetically.

"A million lovers," the third guardian repeated, dreamily.

"That's what she's got," said the first.

"Won't speak to us," growled the second. "Won't say fucking word one."

"Fucking word one," repeated the third, wistfully.

They spoke of Marta. I knew it, despite the obvious lie. What man would have coupled with Marta? What man, even in jest, would have spoken in the same breath of Marta and lust, Marta and jealousy, Marta and sweet concupiscence?

The answer to that question is so obvious I will not even take the space to record it here.

"Five husbands," said the first guardian bitterly, "and a million lovers. And you and you and me unload our pockets there every day."

"Not a wink, not a smile, not a word," said the second.

"She don't even want to serve us," cried the third in some anguish, and for once not merely echoing his friends.

One, two, three, the guardians zipped up.

The third came in my direction. The second turned right around and crossed the street. The first went around the corner of the restaurant.

I determined to question one of the guardians. Not the third, though he was closest. He seemed merely to echo the sentiments of his companions. Not the first, for he was probably already beyond my catching him. But the second, whom I saw walking quickly away on the far side of the street.

I crossed hurriedly and followed him. I didn't want to call out, and I didn't want actually to run—those who dwell in the city are wary of such noise, and after hearing it, the second guardian would not be disposed to stop and talk to me. I wanted, if possible, to ease up behind him, slowly draw abreast, look directly in his eye—to disarm him with my genial aspect—and say "Sir, you and your friends just now—were you speaking of Marta? Do you know her? She interests me strangely."

And he would stop and tell me all he knew of Marta and her life.

The more I knew of Marta the easier it would be to prepare our adventure.

Two full blocks I followed, toward the eastern edge of my neighborhood, into darker streets and past houses more run-down and more boarded-over than those I was mostly familiar with. He lurched and veered drunkenly. If he heard me, he was not disquieted. Or if he was disquieted, it did not show in his gait. When he staggered into a dark, narrow alleyway, he was no more than five meters ahead of me. I hurried forward, catching at a corner of brick to assist me in a final, quick turning.

I heard a noise, like that of a large sack of flour hitting the floor and splitting its thick paper seams.

He, the second guardian, lay at length in the narrow alleyway. The only light was from a streetlamp, somewhere behind me. I stepped a little to the right, so that the light fell upon his face. I saw black blood upon his brow.

Crescented at the second guardian's feet stood five persons, all grinning at me.

Two of them I recognized—the two young women who had jostled me on the street. The one whose hair was bleached stood on the left; the one whose hair was dyed jet stood on the right. Between them were three young men in black trousers, white shirts, and black leather jackets. They did not need to turn around for me to be certain of the winged hourglass insignia. Perhaps even in full daylight I would not have been able to tell the three men apart anyway, but in this quiet dark place, at night, they were wholly indistinguishable to me. They might have been photographic reproductions one of the other.

The young man at the very center of the crescent brought his hand from behind his back and held up a kind of flexible lead weight attached to a wooden grip. It's just the sort of malevolent object that has an innocuous nickname, but I didn't know what it was. *With this*, he would say, *I have rendered the second guardian unconscious.*

The young man at his right knelt down and systematically rifled the guardian's pockets.

The young man at his right knelt down . . .

The girl with the black hair knelt down at the guardian's side, unbuckled his belt, and with a dramatic flourish, pulled it completely free.

The girl with the white hair knelt and wrested off the guardian's shoes.

They stripped him naked. His clothing, as it was removed, was carefully folded and handed to one of the young men who remained standing, with his arms outstretched before him, patient to receive the burden.

They left the guardian his socks.

"Is he dead?" I asked curiously.

All five looked at me then. They smiled. None said anything.

I was suddenly struck with the conviction that all this had been planned and executed for my benefit. The motive itself might still be obscure, but the intention itself was obvious and inescapable.

48

They had no use for his clothing. They had garnered only a few bills of low denomination from his wallet. For so little the guardian might very well be dead.

When I say *For so little*, I do not mean his clothes and his money —I mean whatever it was that they intended to show me by this curious tableau. A tableau it certainly was. There lay the second guardian, naked but for his socks; and there stood his five attackers, reorganized into their careful crescent. The young man from the left still held the guardian's clothing neatly stacked on his outstretched arms.

Their lesson in all this was obscure. I was anxious to know if it were connected somehow with Marta. As I turned the matter over in my mind, I became almost certain it was.

"Do you—" I began, but there was, somewhere behind me, the sound of footsteps.

I glanced down the street. Two men were approaching. When I turned back, the five had disappeared, swallowed by the darkness of the alley.

Instinctively, I hurried after them, deep into the obscurity of that narrow passageway between derelict buildings. I could not see my way at all, but proceeded by dragging my hand along the left-hand wall. The bricks were cold and rough, and the occasional expanses of mortar were crumbling and clammy. Sometimes I flew past brief interstices of superior blackness—these might have been recessed doorways but I did not pause to explore. I turned back once and saw the two men, back-lighted, pausing at the mouth of the alley. I heard their voices, in a foreign tongue, discussing the plight of the second guardian. As one began to stoop over the unfortunate victim, I turned again and plunged deeper into the darkness.

Sometime later, I emerged in another street, well-lighted and unfamiliar. It was in another neighborhood altogether. The five were nowhere in sight. Sticking to thoroughfares and only the best-lighted side streets, I reached home just at midnight.

6

My elation buoyed me up to the third floor of my apartment building. I scarcely needed the stairs.

My entire life, I was convinced, had new purpose and meaning. I didn't foresee all that would come of this chance meeting with Marta in the Baltyk Kitchen—for how could I ever have predicted the infinite ramifications of *that*?—but I knew that things had changed. My brain was awhirl.

I was so excited that I actually, and for the first time ever, forgot the proper sequence of keys and lock-turnings for the door to my flat. I had pressed the keys into the locks in the right sequence, I suppose, but the turns and half-turns had gone awry, and I couldn't get inside. I had to remove the keys and begin again, this time pausing a moment to slow the maelstrom in my head. Those swirling waters gradually calmed to the extent that I was able to get the keys into their locks again and to turn them in the proper sequence: one full turn to the left for the top key, one half turn to the left for the second key, one full turn to the right for the bottom key, and a further half turn to the left for the second key. My three guardians. The door scraped open, and I was inside.

I removed the keys, shut the door, and turned the combination lock carefully, to a cunningly innocuous number.

This lock, on the inside of my door, is set at 1/3/12, the month/day/hour of my birth. It is always locked while I am inside the apartment, even if I have returned intending to remain only a moment. Whenever I go out again, I am forced to retrace that arcana of my birth: 1/3/12. I leave the apartment in the right frame of mind, in mild contemplation of my natal hour. I am better prepared against the adventitious exigencies of the world without.

There is, or there was, a rear door to my flat. It leads, or it led, from the kitchen to a set of wooden stairs at the back of the building. I nailed it shut. I hammered boards over the window. I spilled hot wax into the keyhole. I knifed liquid glue all around the door

The intervening spaces are traversed by corridors.

and stuck it to its frame. I painted it the same color as the wall and set my refrigerator in front of it. There are times, I'm happy to say, when I forget that it's there.

When I've come into my apartment and I've spun my combination lock, I am confident there is no way out, for me or anyone who happens to be there—an unlikely chance, admittedly—without first dialing 1/3/12, the month/day/hour of my birth. That is an acknowledgment of my authority.

My flat is large. It occupies the whole of the fourth floor of my building. I have a living room, a dining room, a kitchen, a bedroom, and a bath. Many apartments in the city have as much to boast of, but my apartment is different from almost every other in that these rooms are not connected to one another directly. Each one exists alone and apart. The intervening spaces are traversed by corridors. Some of these corridors are short and quite wide;

others generously long but absurdly narrow. I've twice as many corridors as I've rooms. Some of the corridors have closets along their length, others have no features at all. One, a fairly short corridor as my corridors go, has three lights in equidistant sconces along the left-hand wall, left-hand that is, going from the dining room toward the kitchen. And another, a fairly long one, from my bedroom to the living room, has no light whatsoever, and as all my doors are on spring hinges and slam shut as soon as I take my hand from the knob, I must move down this particular corridor in total darkness. It is well, I consider, that I have complete faith in the benignity of my apartment toward myself. In such a maze of corridors and with my rooms so widely separated one from the other, there is much latitude for dishonesty and trickery. I might, for instance, easily forget what door leads where. There are so many doors, and as I mentioned, they're on spring hinges. They slam shut. They're always closed. They're identically fashioned, and even I might occasionally mistake them. Yet I never do. When I go to open the door of my bedroom closet, I'm never shocked to find myself walking instead into the corridor that leads to the kitchen. Always I'm greeted with that black vista of my six suits, S-1 through S-6, and nothing else. I'm never disappointed. With so many doors and so many possibilities, I could be driven crazy if things started shifting around. But, as I said, once I've turned that combination lock, the place is irrevocably mine. It has my stamp and seal upon it. It is docile and unrebellious.

For a time, when I first found this place, shortly after I went to work for my Employer, the flat was no more than an agglomeration of empty rooms, empty shelves in empty closets, and this confusing labyrinth of corridors. I slept on the kitchen floor with a bath towel for a pillow. I covered the windows with brown paper. I hung one suit in every room, so that no room would forget that it was I who inhabited the place. I needed furniture I decided, but I didn't want to buy it. It wasn't a question of money, really, though at the time I had but little. But I knew, from sad experience, that furniture is resentful of purchase. Furniture prefers a trial of use before it is signed over. Ownership is a two-way street. If I had gone out and simply bought a bed, I might have been displeased with it. Perhaps the headboard would have been too low, or the footboard too far away, or the mattress too soft, or the springs too loud. And quite as possibly, the bed might have been displeased with me: I might have been too tall or too heavy, or I might have thrashed about in my sleep, or perhaps the bed would have had no view from the position in which I set it. (I do not in fact think that this would have been the case, for I am of a model height and weight, I do not move at all in my sleep, and my bedroom has adequate views from every point; but a bed, in a furniture showroom, would know nothing of this and would keep its trepidations.) All of which is to say that I went out and leased five rooms of furniture from a store, quite nearby, which specialized in such accommodations. If I did not get along with the furniture, or if the furniture did not get along with me, then no harm would have been done. I would simply have the five rooms returned, an annulment of a doomed marriage.

I chose Early American, because that was the only style in which five complete rooms were available. I had no wish to mix genres. To move from a living room into a dining room is an experience sufficiently jarring in its very nature, without having also to deal with a revolution in interior decoration as well.

In the showroom I was careful to say, in quite a loud voice, for the reassurance of the furniture, "I don't want to buy. I only want to lease, to take the pieces on trial." This, I think, got us off to a good start, and, as it happened, I chose well. The furniture suited me perfectly. I evidently suited it. For two years I forwarded my payments according to the terms of the lease. Then one day, as I happened to walk past the store, I noticed a "Going Out of Business" banner taped in the window. I suspected this was no more than an advertising ploy, in which old, inflated prices were touted as new and reduced, but when I returned that way the following week, I saw that indeed, the store had been closed. I stopped sending in my monthly check and suspected that something would happen. I'd receive a notice that my lease had been turned over to Such and So Company for collection, or a van would pull up before my building and reclaim all five rooms. But nothing happened. My lease was perhaps lost in the shuffling out. Or, Early American having fallen decidedly out of public favor, my five rooms were not thought worth the bother of reclamation.

But whatever happened out there, nothing at all happened inside my apartment. The five rooms of Early American became all mine, in this sidling manner. The furniture itself sensed the alteration in actual ownership, I think. It appreciated the subtle and unstraightforward manner in which this was accomplished. Bills of sale are ugly crass things, and this transference was accomplished slowly and without any jerks. All five rooms seemed to shiver a little in their new identity—like a cobbler's boy who, after five years of what he imagines to be voluntary apprenticeship, suddenly catches sight, for the first time, of his indenture papers at the bottom of a trunk—and then to settle in for good. After that I had to go through the whole apartment and rearrange the pictures on the wall. Each had come little askew on its wire—a final, obscure gesture of independence.

When I went into the kitchen, I was surprised to see, set out on the counter, all the ingredients for a meal I had planned for myself this evening—less of course the one spice that had been wanting, a lack that became the linchpin for all that tumbled down afterwards. How paltry it all looked, how insignificant! Rather than return those bags and boxes and jars to their proper shelves, I shoveled them all into the trash. That was an extravagant gesture and needlessly wasteful, I know, but I needed to mark the importance of the evening. After all, if I had found that particular spice, I would have returned home without untoward incident, prepared that simple dish, eaten it in quiet, and never known of the existence of Marta of the Baltyk Kitchen. At nine o'clock, I would very likely have been sitting in the dining room, contemplating the remains of that very dish, when Marta herself walked by on the sidewalk outside. I trembled thinking how close I had come to the maintenance of such criminal ignorance.

The cookbook open on the corner, I did not throw it away, though I did rip out the page that contained the recipe I had wanted to make. That I burned with one of the wooden matches I use to light the gas burners on the range. I replaced the cookbook, suddenly dear to me above all others I owned because of that missing page, back on the shelf in its proper, alphabetical by author, place. It was on the seventh shelf, twelfth from the end.

I have many cookbooks, twelve shelves of them, in fact, which I keep in the short wide corridor that leads from the kitchen to the bathroom. I have no books other than these. If for some reason a book other than a cookbook comes into my possession, I destroy it. I have no compunction when it comes to fiction, history, and philosophical speculation. Fiction I tend to burn, history I simply discard, philosophical speculation I rip to shreds, signature by signature.

I prepared a tray and took it into the dining room. On the tray were a glass, a bottle of milk, a spoon, and a container of chocolate sauce. I poured the glass of milk and then placed a spoonful of chocolate into my mouth. I drank down a third of the glass of milk and mixed the two within my mouth until it had become the exact replication of the chocolate milk which is the single pleasant memory of the dreary and painful length of my childhood. The milk is very white, the chocolate is very nearly black. I do not like to mix them in the glass, where the mixture suffuses to a murky, characterless brown. I will do that only in my mouth, where the dilution of the white and black takes place in darkness and where the mixture is swallowed without my ever seeing the diminution of the colors' integrity. I performed this comforting ritual twice more until the milk in the glass was gone, and then I returned the tray to the kitchen.

I had no thought of going to bed. In the first place, I need very little sleep. Long ago, I weaned myself from the need of it, in quarter-hour increments. Night after night, quarter-hour by quarter-hour, I slept less and less. At three and three-quarter hours I hit a kind of plateau. Perhaps I might have gone further —indeed, I have no doubt that I might have gone further—but I did not see the need. To sleep for such a time is a pleasant, earned recreation, and I sleep the sleep of the happy dead; but even a quarter-hour longer would be a sickly self-indulgence.

I am left, in consequence, with a great deal of time on my hands. But I am self-sufficient, a world unto myself, and not one moment of that time is wasted. I come home from work, I prepare dinner, and this is often a long and complicated process in itself. Afterwards, I perform certain tasks. I do work I've brought home from the office, and I clean the house. I am very particular about both activities. I am not required to bring work home from the office, but it pleases me to do so. I need no other reason. I am currently reworking, in careful and fine India ink, a careless and pencilled set of books from many years back, kept by my Employer for a customer who has since gone bankrupt. My Employer, should he know of this task, would doubtless consider that it was unnecessary and might even reprimand me for having slipped the ledger out of its particular place on the storeroom shelves; but any job is worth doing well, and a job well done redounds to the credit of the one who accomplished it.

Simply because my life was fraught with new significance and infused with new purpose was an insufficient reason for abandoning my routine. I sat down at the desk that is pushed against the long living room wall, and I copied out two weeks of entries in my finest, carefullest hand. When I was through, exactly eighty-six minutes later, I blotted the last page and then glanced back at all that I had done in the past few months. That work was indistinguishable from the work I had done tonight, though I was, I was certain, a man entirely altered in form and purpose. That I had maintained my prowess with my pen, that I had not allowed my talents to be diverted by the nervous energy that infused me, was added proof of the *rightness* of my decision to press Marta toward her eagerly sought death.

I closed the original ledger, with its pencil-smeared, dog-eared pages. I placed it atop the new ledger, with its crisp rag leaves indelibly and beautifully filled with India ink entries. I had executed thousands of graceful characters and numerals along perfectly executed ruled lines, without a single blot.

I looked up into the mirror that hangs on the wall behind the desk. "Without a single blot," I told myself aloud.

It is not to be wondered at. I am, myself, the perfect human specimen. The mirror told me so, as did my self-portrait which hangs above the hearth mantel. I am one hundred eighty centimeters in height, of a pleasing medium build with natural musculature. I was born with blue eyes. They are, I assume, still of that hue. I have black hair and white skin and perfect white teeth. My features are regular in a most uncommon way. I draw strength from the mirrors, from the intensification of what I see thrown back at myself. I have at least one mirror in every room, and in most rooms there are two or even more. I have mirrors of all various sizes and in all manner of shapes and in a variety of frames. Mirrors, it is not commonly known, have textures. A mirror throws reality back in a way peculiar to itself. A man, looking at himself in two mirrors hung side by side on a wall, will see two entirely different men gazing back at him in astonishment at the difference. I am aware of this peculiarity of mirrors, but it affects me little. When I look into my many mirrors, I am shown, always, slightly varying pictures of my own perfection. This is anything but disconcerting.

Marta, I was certain, had not a single mirror in her flat. Her windows were shaded at night so that the glass panes would not chance to throw her reflection back in her eyes. Would Medusa turn to stone if she gazed into a mirror? Polished surfaces Marta covered with clothes or sprinkled with powder. All her cookware was cast-iron, against the chance of reflection. All the pictures on her walls were framed without glass.

I was, I saw then, slipping deeper into Marta's life.

7

I found myself at work the following morning.

I write those words carefully and with precision. That is to say, I found myself at work without recollection of having waked, evacuated, cleansed myself, dressed, drunk chocolate, spun my combination lock, descended my stairs, or traversed the sidewalks and the streets from my apartment, Number FORTY-SEVEN, to my Employer's office. I have not, it is true, trained my memory to savor this unvarying week-daily routine. Occasionally, indeed, my memory may slickly pass over one or the other of these varied elements, but to have lost all of them on a single day seemed more than careless.

I found myself that morning standing behind my desk, my back to the tall windows, facing a wall of empty shelving. I seated myself at my desk, and tried to reason it out.

I was distracted immediately by the feel of the chilled smooth curved wood beneath me. The last thing I remembered was slipping into bed. Perhaps I was asleep even before I had pulled the spread up under my neck. But the next sensation after that one was of sliding along the polished wood of the seat of the swivel chair in my office. I had never connected those two sensations.

I sat very still at my desk, unwilling that other sensations should crowd in upon me before I had had the opportunity to recapture what had been taken away. I closed my eyes. I placed my hands over my ears. I trembled with the realization that I did not even know the number of the suit I was wearing. I could not remember having consulted my schedule of sartorial propriety. I might, for all I knew at that moment, be wearing the wrong suit. I twitched some muscles at various points of my anatomy to see how they responded to the fiber of the suit. Because of a certain stretch over my left breast, because of a slight tension on the inside of my left thigh, I conjectured that I was encased in Suit S-1. I did not open my eyes to see. To have been wrong would have unmanned me.

I went over my week-daily routine in my fevered brain and attempted to trick myself into believing that I was remembering the events of that morning. Yet I knew I was only mechanically reviewing a cherished itinerary. The pattern in my hot brain was cold. It had the texture only of ice. Three times I went over the week-daily routine in my mind, desperately searching for the one detail that would distinguish this morning from every other morning. That detail would not present itself.

It was as I began the fourth cycle, however, that I realized suddenly the *motive* behind my forgetfulness. I knew, with an unerrable certainty, *why* these hours of the early morning had been erased from my consciousness.

In my mind, on the fourth cold iteration of my week-daily routine, I waked up, as I always do, with my fingers curved around the edge of the spread. As I always do, I carefully rolled the spread back toward my feet, sitting up gradually as I did so. I turned myself out of the bed and stood upon the bare bedroom floor. I knew I performed these actions every morning, you see, and my memory of doing them yesterday morning—the day I met Marta—was quite clear and distinct. I could recall, for instance, of yesterday morning, that the floor was colder than I had anticipated its being. A single detail such as that distinguished that day from all others in my mind.

But of this morning, nothing at all.

Every morning I went directly to the bathroom and evacuated my bowels. This I did, in my mind, for the fourth time, hoping nearly against hope for a single detail to bring the whole sequence back to me. If, for instance, I remembered some peculiarity of my stool this morning, then I was certain that all the other sensations would flood back in upon me. Yet, in my mind, as I arranged myself to stand above the toilet and examine my stool, I saw nothing but a kind of paradigm of stool—a dictionary drawing—prototypical but lifeless. Not any sort of stool to auger by.

And *that* was the answer.

That was the reason why my mind had blanked on the entire morning.

Someone—whether my unconscious self or another being altogether—wished me to forget the appearance of my stool that morning. The dis-remembering of everything else had been merely a blind, as a clever murderer will hide his one true victim among twenty-three others he does in quite at random and casually. That is to say, it did not really matter whether I recalled choosing my morning's suit, or could bring to mind how deeply I thrust the spoon into my box of chocolate, or how many persons begged me for money on the way to work—but on the day following my vow to assist Marta in her heart-wish of death, the condition of my stool would be of supreme importance.

Yet I could remember nothing of that morning's evacuation.

A certain recognizable hollowness below the waist told me it had occurred quite as usual, but the details of the business remained agonizingly beyond my grasp. With my eyes shut and my hands over my ears, I tried to construct some possibilities of appearance in the stool, but that was a fruitless task. Tiresias never augered from imaginary entrails. The guts were hot, bloody, and steaming that he wound about his arms and pressed against his cracked lips.

I came quickly to the only possible conclusion: that this was to be a day of consummate importance in my life. Without the evidence of my stool, of course, it would be impossible to predict in what manner the importance would evidence itself. I knew better, of course, than to imagine, on the one extreme of good fortune, a lottery win when I did not even purchase tickets; or, on the other, a black safe falling upon my head from a tenth-floor window, when there were no buildings in this neighborhood so high as that. No, the importance would be manifested in some manner other than *good fortune* or *bad fortune*. It might, for instance, be a sudden turning of my mind, in a direction so new and surprising I would have been previously unaware of the existence of such a point on my mental compass. Or it might, I could conceive, be the precise and correct plan for shuffling Marta out of this vale of hot tears. But, most probably, I told myself, it would be something I did not expect at all.

That is the way of auguries.

That is the way of life itself.

The office where I work is in the neighborhood that borders on my own, to the south. The office occupies the entire fourth floor of a narrow brick building with a much weathered cast-iron front. Similar buildings, but much larger, hem it in on both sides. On the floors below my Employer's offices are three small independent firms. One of them is involved in some way with textiles, for scraps of cloth are baled out in front of the building every evening when I leave work. Another of them is involved, I conjecture, in the construction of furniture, for I hear saws and hammers when the elevator passes that door. The third appears to be a storage facility, for I see cartons taken in and out of the building nearly constantly, and the elevator is stuck at that floor for long and inconvenient periods of time.

The floor above us is ostensibly empty, although now and again, when the radiator is quiet and my Employer is not coughing, I hear a surreptitious footpad above me, and now and again, when I look out one of the vast grimy windows at the back of the loft—for it is that, and nothing else—I see some object drop past. But I'm always so startled by its appearance there and it falls so quickly, that I'm at a loss to make out exactly what it is. Even when I've heard it crash below and looked out of the window, I'm unable to distinguish the fallen object from the detritus in the courtyard in back. But whatever it was, I know it must have been flung from one of the windows directly above.

The loft is long and narrow, with tall grimy windows at either end. The floors are of dark-stained woods, macerated, slightly rolling. The walls are brick, the ceiling is of patterned tin. There are, here and there, iron support poles, cunningly molded like narrow acanthus palms. In corners and along the walls are pipes of varying thickness, emerging through holes in the floor and disappearing into holes in the ceiling. Sometimes I catch a glimpse of a shred of wall in the loft below—the storage loft—if I stand just so. If I look up however, I see nothing but blackness in the loft above. These are waste pipes and heating pipes and water pipes, I suppose. They knock loudly. Water rushes through them in torrents. They give off heat sometimes, at other times a clammy chilliness. My Employer has erected a few partitions, giving himself a large office at the back, and me a small office at the front. In between are my Employer's files, his duplicating machine, his punchers, his posting machines, his boxes of supplies, and his dictionaries.

My Employer trusts me to do my work. He does not check up on me constantly. I go to his office and nod to him upon my arrival in the morning—if he is there before me. If I arrive first, he pokes his head around my partition and nods at me. Since we are infrequently visited and the floor above is ostensibly uninhabited, the elevator rarely rises above the third floor. My Employer suffers. He does not smoke, but he has a smoker's cough. It is as loud as the jackhammer that once tore up the street outside my window. My Employer limps, sometimes on his left leg, and sometimes on his right. He does not drink, but he suffers from gout. Even in the worst weather, I've seen him in nothing but the softest slippers. His wife is dead, and he's told me on more than one occasion that he has no interest in sex, but I have reason to believe he is syphilitic. My Employer does not have a secretary. He answers his own telephone. He types his own letters. He makes his own tea. I am his sole Employee, and many days go by in which we speak not a word to one another. In the storeroom between our offices, there is a rickety table, painted bright red. If my Employer wants me to do some work he puts it on that table, and eventually I find it. When I've done that work, I put it back on the table, and eventually my Employer picks it up again. He never gives me specific instructions as to what I'm to do, but by dint of practice and instinct, I am invariably correct in following his wishes. Sometimes when he goes out, I wander to the back of the loft and look out the windows there. It's on those occasions I see things that have been hurled out of the windows of the ostensibly empty loft above. I pick up items on my Employer's desk, and then I put them down again, exactly in the same place. I go through his files and read his correspondence. I count the pencils in his desk drawer and test their sharpness with the tip of my thumb.

In the block of buildings behind are more lofts, some of them given over to business, some of them to storage, and some of them actually inhabited. I sometimes stand at the back windows and look out at the habited lofts as I read my Employer's correspondence or count his pencils. Now and then I see a man in the loft directly across the way. He wears a short white kimono with large black Oriental characters painted on it. I call him Karl.

Most of the time, however, I'm at the front of the loft, in my office. My windows look out onto the street. Directly across is a large, newish office building housing some department of the city government. I could, if I wished, stare into the city workers' offices all day long, but I do not, and they have the courtesy to ignore me as well. The street itself is narrow and littered.

At this time of which I speak, directly below and just beyond the door of my building, was an abandoned car with its front wheel over the edge of the curb. Six alcoholic men had taken up residence in the automobile in the previous week, three in the front seat and three in the back. Every morning they wakened just as I came into the office. But every day as well, I noted that another part of the car was wanting: a hubcap, a windshield wiper, the back bumper. It was my first duty in the morning to telephone the police and have them remove the six drunks, and it was the police, I suspect, who removed some portion of the automobile as they shooed away the derelicts. It would be only a

Six alcoholic men had taken up residence in the automobile.

matter of a few weeks until the six drunks were deprived of their home altogether. I experienced a curious satisfaction in watching the automobile disappear piecemeal.

I do my work at my desk, with my back to the window. My office is illumined by the sun. I do not like fluorescent light. Now and then when the heat comes on unexpectedly and the office in a matter of minutes is suffused with hot steamy air from the hissing pipes, I'll have to stand up and open one of my tall windows. I see derelicts and unhappy women and policemen on the sidewalk below. I see trucks angled up over the curb, loading or unloading cartons from the storage loft directly below. I hear voices in half a dozen foreign languages I can neither understand nor even identify. The city office workers in their yellow-lighted offices ignore me, and I ignore them.

Howard is our only regular visitor. Howard is the Delivery

Boy for the pharmacy two streets over. He brings my Employer's medicine. Howard comes at least three times a week, and during inclement seasons, once or even twice a day. Howard and I have exchanged words on several occasions, an intimacy in itself something of a marvel, for I am not accustomed to speech. I have no interest in making the acquaintance of shop boys. Yet Howard interests me, both in his character as our most frequent visitor and in his position as one who makes deliveries. He must see the interiors of many offices and many flats. In the doorway of how many living rooms has Howard stood, I ask myself frequently. Into how many lives has Howard Dormin entered, albeit in the most peripheral fashion? Has he been affected by this wide experience with the apartments and offices of total strangers?

I do not understand how he could help but be affected. The accumulated wisdom of a Delivery Boy must, by the very nature of his peripatetic employment, be greater than that of a young man who is confined to a place behind a counter or, it might be, a desk.

I must also admit yet a third reason for my indulgence toward this young man. Sometimes, in the course of the day, I may hear no other voice but his speak in English.

8

"Fucking Nazis!" Howard shouted as the elevator door shrieked open. He held a transistor radio to his ear and shook it. "Fucking Nazis! They ruined my radio!"

He saw me. "Did you see that?" he said angrily. Howard's not tall, and he isn't fat. His skin's not good, and his clothes don't fit. He probably isn't as young as he looks. "Did you see what the Nazis did to my radio?"

"Could it be the battery?" I asked. I don't often speak, but I was moved by Howard's evident distress.

"Fucking Nazis," Howard breathed, "fucking around with my radio."

He had brought medicine for my Employer. My Employer was out so I took the package and put it on his desk. My hand was still on the package when something brown and square fell past the window and landed with a noise of shattering glass on the blind courtyard pavement below.

Howard was right behind me.

"Did you see what it was?" I asked.

"Fucking Nazis up there," said Howard definitely and pointed to the ostensibly empty loft above. "Throwing shit out the fucking window. Destroying innocent people on the ground."

I went to the window and raised it. The ledge was caked with pigeon stool, uninterpretable even in such mass. Howard and I leaned out. I couldn't make out, in the heap of detritus below, what had been thrown out of the window above.

Howard hurled his radio against the back wall of the building opposite. It shattered and spilled down the bricks. Karl came to his window and mouthed imprecations at us. As Karl raised his window, I lowered my Employer's.

Howard and I went to the front of the loft. I see Howard frequently—as frequently as I see anyone in the world actually, except my Employer—but we rarely talk at any length. I offered Howard a cup of coffee, but he had brought his own.

I sat behind my desk. Howard sat behind me, perched on the window ledge. Over my shoulder, he complained about his job, which was neither more nor less than delivering small packages for the pharmacist two streets over.

"Fucking cows," he said darkly. "Old cows always trying to kiss me. They say to me, 'You from the pharmacist?' I say, 'Yes.' They say, 'I can't get up. Bring it in the bedroom.' So I fight my way to the bedroom. Old cows lying in wait, jump on my back, kiss me. What's a man for? Just to kiss old cows? I got this trick, see? I learned how to vomit. Any time. Like there's a trigger in my throat. Old cow wants to kiss me, I let her, see. I let her get her lips up to mine, and I pull the trigger. Pull the trigger, and vomit on the old cow's mouth. I say 'Sorry, I guess I got sick.' Then their whole place stinks, and they got to move out 'cause the whole place stinks like my vomit forever. Fucking cow tries to kiss me, she's got to find a new place to live. That's revenge."

Howard's conversation didn't please me. I knew it wouldn't. It never had before. There had been no reason to believe that this day's exchange would be pleasanter. And yet I had asked him to talk to me. I wanted something from him. I had the feeling when I first saw him in the elevator, shaking the defunct radio at his ear, that Howard would be of some use to me. I wasn't sure how. Time and circumstance would show that. I let him talk on. He sipped loudly at his coffee behind me. He was bored, I could sense that. I wasn't used to talking to people. I didn't know how to make Howard feel at ease. I tried to think of something to say.

I said, "If you don't like the job, why do you stay in it?"

"Big tips," said Howard.

I gave him a small bill.

He seemed disposed to linger.

"Shitty job," he remarked after a while. He crushed his coffee cup.

"What would you rather do?"

"Join the army," he said.

"Why don't you?" I asked. "The army's frequently recruiting."

"Tried," said Howard. "Wouldn't let me in. I was too smart. Broke all their fucking rating machines when I took their fucking tests. That was it. Too smart. I saw too much. I saw the right answers like they was written in the margins. Broke the fucking machines. Army sent me a bill for breaking their goddamn fucking rating machines, I said, 'You let me in, and you take the money out of my paycheck.'"

Howard took a walk around my office. He picked up the things on my desk. He was restless again, but I didn't want to let him go yet. I had the feeling that I was supposed to learn something from him, or more precisely, I sensed that he had been sent there to *tell* me something and only waited for the password to deliver his message. My Employer's medicine was only a blind. I was afraid he'd go without telling me what it was needful for me to know. Moreover, I had to get him to speak before my Employer returned, and my Employer was expected back at any moment.

"Malcontent," I said, hoping that was the code word. "Lettuce. Punctual."

Howard shook his head slowly. I hadn't guessed right. "Got to move on," he said.

I couldn't let him leave. Frantically, I said the first thing that came into my head: "What do you know about that gang?"

"What gang?" he asked quickly, and turned and looked at me closely.

I smiled with the certain knowledge that I had asked the right question. I had guessed the code words.

"The gang with the hourglass on their jackets."

Howard said nothing, but he had stopped moving about the room.

"The hourglass with wings," I said.

"The Fuggits," said Howard.

"Tempus Fugit," I corrected.

"They're called the Fuggits," Howard said, as if I'd said nothing. "That who you mean?"

I nodded. "Two women..."

"Shade and Shadow," said Howard.

"Three men," I said.

"Clay, Dust, and Ashes," said Howard.

"What do you know about them?" I asked.

"Nothing," said Howard.

"I saw them attack a man last night," I said. "They took off all his clothes and left him in an alleyway."

Howard said nothing. He went to the window and looked out of it.

"The Fuggits?" I said. "You're certain?"

"Come to my house tomorrow," said Howard. "Meet my grandfather."

"I don't know where you live," I said.

Howard took a map out of his pocket and marked his address with a black circle. He lived in another, but nearby, neighborhood.

"I work on Saturday," I said.

"Come after work," said Howard and left.

My Employer didn't return for some time. I needn't have hurried so with the code word.

The remainder of the day was uneventful, yet the emptiness of those hours reverberated with purpose and with meaning for me. Howard, I was convinced, was a Messenger. Whose I did not know. His message I could not conceive, but I was confident of receiving it on Saturday night when I visited him in his home—or in that place Howard in this venture had been instructed to call his home. I was proud that I had found him out. Not every one passing such a man as Howard Dormin on the street would have picked out his essential identity as a Messenger. His instructions, no doubt, had been to feel me out, to discover whether my discernment was sufficient, my instincts up to the mark. They were, most evidently, for Howard had scheduled another and obviously private meeting.

At his house, I was persuaded, I would discover what I needed to know.

My Employer returned. I continued to work on the tasks he had set out for me. Every once in a while I went to my window and looked down into the street, just in case there was something there I would want to be apprised of. Gradually, the trash and leavings of the manufacturing concerns in the lofts below us began to build up outside—barrels of sawdust, wired bales of fabric scraps, boxes of synthetic stuffing—until the sidewalk was nearly impassable with it. I sometimes wished that some of the workers spoke English so that I might discover, at last, what it was that was actually done in those lower lofts. If finished products of some description were ever taken out of those lofts and loaded into trucks. I never recognized them as such. There was something, I think I may say, sinister in all this, but the workers never bothered my Employer or me, and the police never came with guns.

Below on the sidewalk, I watched a woman, about sixty years of age I should say, with a little hat and a clasped purse, as she moved what was apparently her whole household. She had six large suitcases, as many shopping bags, two wooden crates of manageable size, three hat boxes tied up, and a couple of cardboard cartons secured with twine. She moved them by hand, one by one, eight feet at a time, building up one heap of belongings to the west as she diminished her previous heap to the east. It reminded me of a mathematical game called the Pyramids of Luxor. That morning on the way to work, I remembered having passed her, but then she stood still, with her purse clasped before her, and I assumed she waited for a cab. As the day wore on, she moved from one end of the block to the other, but where she had come from and where she was going, I had no idea. When I left my Employer's office late that afternoon, squeezing my way along the sidewalk between the wired bales of fabric scraps and the pyramided stacks of synthetic stuffing, I passed her again. A truck driver, his van empty, had stopped and asked if he couldn't transport the things for her in his truck—it would be no problem, he assured her—but the woman berated him as ungentlemanly for approaching her without being properly introduced.

I was glad of this momentary distraction. It made me realize that this was not a normal day and that I should not pursue my normal course home. Anyway, the previous day's events had altered my whole life. My old ways and courses would no longer serve. I should not, I told myself, simply return directly home by my former, well-trodden path. For one thing, I did not want to pass the grocery that had begun this adventure with its false sign:

DEATH IN THE FAMILY

For another, I was certain that I had already accomplished what was required of me that day—I had seen Howard, I had subtly informed Howard that I saw through his disguise to his essential identity as a Messenger, I had accepted his invitation to a meeting. I felt, in short, that I had done my duty and that I ought to be rewarded for it. I decided to visit Annie.

I turned the corner suddenly and headed for the neighborhood where Annie works. It is close by, but entirely to be distinguished from, on the one hand, the neighborhood where I work and, on the other hand, the neighborhood where I live. It is quite distinct, moreover, from the neighborhood where Annie has her own flat.

Annie works in one of those areas made up entirely of vast city office buildings interspersed with such businesses as cater to the diurnal needs of city workers—cheap restaurants, stalls that provide umbrellas in rainy weather and sunglasses in clement, musty card shops, and shoe stores dealing in slightly damaged imports. Single-handedly Annie runs one of those small places that produce photographic prints in a matter of hours. Office workers drop exposed film off on the way to work and pick up the finished prints on their way home. Annie therefore has long hours, arriving well before the city offices are open and leaving only when the city offices are closed and the entire neighborhood appears deserted.

The shop is small, with wide plate-glass windows. Annie stands at a counter in the back, with lozenged shelves behind her —rather like wineracks—holding boxes of unexposed film for purchase. In front of the shop are two large machines, cumbersome and steely, which in one long sequence develop a roll of film, wash the negatives, and expose them to produce a long roll of colorful prints, which then—in equally ingenious manner— are snipped off by a knife operating by means of an electric eye. The two machines are arranged in the front windows so that the still wet rolls of photographic prints can be seen unrolling out of the bowels of the machine, thin, narrow, colorful tongues that speak with a wrenching eloquence of the banality of city office workers' lives.

Before going inside Annie's shop, I always stand outside for a few minutes, watching these rolls of photographs rolling by in stately, inexorable procession. I am thrilled by this undeserved insight into the lives of strangers. I imagine myself Howard, hovering on the threshold of a strange apartment, gazing at a tableau formulated by my ringing of the doorbell. Here, in Annie's domain, are more tableaux, rectangular, regular, colored, smiling, silent, and dead.

My lingering before the window also gives Annie the opportunity to note my presence and to prepare herself to receive me.

I do not admire the mass of women. I find the ideal of beauty defined and perpetuated by advertisements and photographs of movie stars in popular magazines to be a kind of grotesquerie so pronounced that I can scarcely believe that it is not a deliberate joke. Annie's style of beauty is distinctly different from this absurd norm. She is shorter than I. Her figure is gooselike and voluptuous. Her hips are wide, and her feet are dainty. Her hair is black, her skin an unblemished cream. Her lips and nails are painted red. Her smile is a sneer, and her black eyes are contemptuous. I appreciate her fully, but for the most of men, her beauty is of a nature too peculiar, prickly, and cactuslike to be desired with the whole of the heart and loins.

Annie wears a beauty mark, and by that mark I read her like a book. If it lies directly above her left eye, she is having a good day, in general. If it lies directly above her right eye, she is very much in the mood for masculine company. (In the past five months, two weeks, and two days, *I* am synonymous with *masculine company*. I am convinced Annie desires no one but me.) If the mark is affixed below her right eye, her mood is foul. I have seen it below her left eye only once, and that was the day she told me that her mother had died.

This day the mark, particularly black, was above her right eye, as I hoped it would be.

She smiled at me through the window. As if she had known I was coming by, she wore a white blouse with large black polka dots, and white pants with long black stripes. The stripes were wide at her hips, but they tapered down to mere black lines at her tiny ankles.

I went into the shop. A customer stood at the counter, looking through prints. From beneath the counter Annie took a small white package and pushed it across the surface of the counter toward me.

"I have something for you," she said.

I took up the package and opened it. Inside were perhaps two dozen photographic prints, grainy and so dim in respect to color that they appeared entirely black-and-white to me. I flipped through them quickly at first and then more slowly examined them one by one. In the photographs, two men and a woman performed a variety of athletic sexual acts on a long living room couch, on a narrow bed, and braced against a bathroom sink. The last photograph showed the three of them, naked but for some improbable leather *accoutrements*, standing in the kitchen, making flapjacks on a black range.

"I think you've made a mistake," said I to Annie after a few minutes, slipping the photographs back into their envelope, "these are not mine."

"Sorry," said Annie and put the photographs back under the counter.

The single customer departed.

Annie said, "That was the only decent set that came in today. I

The last photograph showed the three of them . . .

don't even know if they're worth keeping a duplicate of."

"I'd like a print of the kitchen scene," I said.

Annie had still an hour of work before she could leave. I asked if I could visit her at her apartment later. She agreed to my proposal but said, "Don't come until eleven. My mother and father are visiting me, and their train doesn't leave until then."

I acquiesced to this, but I recalled that Annie had once told me that her mother was dead. In fact, her mother's death had been Annie's excuse for disappearing from the city for three days the previous February. On another occasion, in March, Annie had told me that her mother had instituted divorce proceedings against her father, citing adultery as the cause. I did not see fit to point out these inconsistencies in Annie's family history. They were as much a part of her as her goosey bust or her delicate ankles.

9

I walked home from Annie's place of business, through the deepening twilight, along a route that was tolerably familiar to me. Nothing untoward occurred. I saw nothing but what I was accustomed to seeing. I heard nothing but what I was accustomed to hear.

At home I went into my bedroom and took off my suit, S-4, brushed it, folded the trousers, slipped the jacket onto a wooden hanger and replaced it in the narrow closet that contains nothing but my six suits, S-1 through S-6. There is room enough there, though the closet is quite small, for other things. I might easily, for instance, have hung my six white shirts there alongside the suits—or even have used the shirts as white dividers. But the shirts are folded in the third drawer of my dresser. They are unnumbered, and I wear them quite at random. I might have placed on the floor of the closet my six pairs of black wing-tip shoes, for the boards there are completely bare. But my shoes are lined up beneath the foot of my bed. I might have placed my black socks in a shoe box on the shelf above the rack, but my socks are bundled in the top drawer of my dresser. I might have hung my slender black ties on a hanger pushed right against the side of the closet wall, or set on a hook that was already screwed into the back of the door, but my ties hang over one of the long bolts that holds my dresser mirror in place. The closet is empty but for my suits S-1 through S-6.

My Employer believes that I have but one suit and that I wear it day in and day out. I have told him that this is not so. I have explained, truthfully, that though the suits may appear identical, there are minute—and to my eyes, quite obvious—differences. The width of a lapel, the stitching in a sleeve lining, the pattern of buttons on a cuff—any one of these things will instantly declare the particular number of the suit to me, were I ever to forget which I had put on in the morning.

I have a schedule I've worked out in a small leather-bound notebook that lets me know which suit it is appropriate to wear

There is room enough there, though the closet is quite small ...

on a particular day. It is a kind of perpetual calendar of sartorial propriety. The system I worked out is complicated and not of issue here. I ought perhaps simply to say that it is infinitely more subtle than, say, S-1 is to be worn on Monday, S-2 on Tuesday, and so on through S-6 on Saturday, with Sunday's slack taken up by S-1 through S-6 in turn. Such a system as that would be merely rude, mechanical, and far beneath my dignity.

S-4 is undoubtedly my favorite. I had denied to myself for a long while that this was the case. I should not, I argued, allow myself to be swayed toward a liking of one suit at the expense of all the others. I shouldn't have a scale of preference. Yet I did and eventually came to see that this is the natural order of things. Of any six items, bearing a greater or smaller similarity, one will be the best, one will be the worst, and the other four will somehow arrange themselves in between. So with a litter of rodents, so with a closet of suits. I preferred S-4, not for any reason so obvious as *The pockets are cut well* or *Its length in the back is precisely right*, but simply because I felt better when I had it on.

That I had encountered Marta while wearing S-4 was needlessly added proof of the viability of my preference.

I thought then of Marta's clothing saturated with her essence. Did she wash her clothing in a small stained sink in her flat? Or did she send her clothing out to some establishment in the neighborhood? Did she, I shuddered to consider, have her uniforms cleaned at the place where I took my suits? On automated racks, did her shapeless dresses thrash their hems and sleeves against my trousers and jackets? Had Marta, in this subtle manner, already affected me?

I returned to my closet, stepped inside, and shut the door behind me. I was alone with my suits. I breathed deeply. I did not smell Marta. I closed my eyes and touched the sleeves of all my jackets. My fingers did not touch her.

I emerged from the closet, relieved. But I vowed that I would give my custom to no more cleaning establishments in the immediate neighborhood. I would take my six suits far away, to guard against the possibility of contact and contagion.

I prepared a small dinner for myself, washed up, and estimated the time by the position of the moon. I had yet another two hours before my appointment with Annie.

I wondered at first whether I ought not simply walk around the neighborhood for a while but then remembered how frequently in the immediate past I had been taken unawares. Nothing was to be gained and much might be lost, if I simply wandered the streets in a distracted, receptive mood. I might be attacked by the gang, for instance. I might find a dead man in an alleyway and be forced to give evidence at a police station. On a deserted stretch of street I might come across Marta herself. I determined to remain in my flat. To occupy this interval profitably, I determined that I would do a little cleaning.

There is a method in my manner of cleaning. I could not be satisfied with any superficial dusting, polishing, waxing, rubbing, shining, scraping, slicking, and scouring. After so cursory a regimen, over the five rooms and the numberless corridors every night, a casual visitor might be struck by the overall cleanliness of the place, but I would view it as only a whited sepulchre, bright on the outside and corrupt within. I would know, if I cleaned as others were content to clean, that the real filth lay hidden on surfaces I did not in the normal course of things see. It roped itself longer and longer through the grid of linoleum squares in the kitchen. It secreted itself in the crannies on the undersides of large pieces of furniture, smugly secure and obscenely propagating. The sickly sweet breath of putrescence was exhaled in corners where the casual mop, broom, pan, cloth, towel, trowel, duster, besom, sponge, and Hoover never reached or even thought of.

I work room by room and corridor by corridor. A corridor, depending on its length and width, may take no more than three or four days. A room will require at least seven. If I spend less than seven evenings on a room, I cannot allow myself to believe it really clean.

I am thorough.

A once-around of the whole flat requires, on the average, between nine and ten weeks. I will have to say, however, that I take far greater pleasure in cleaning a room than a corridor. There is a difference not so much in scale as in intrinsic interest. It is only natural, I think, that I should enjoy the greater variety of a living room or a kitchen or a bath or a bedroom or a dining room, more than the scant variations that may be picked out of a simple corridor. Therefore, in recognition of the importance of this period to my life, I might have wished that my schedule had placed me in one of the more interesting rooms—the living room perhaps, or even the bath. But despite my inward elation, I did not alter my schedule. A more indulgent man than I might have said to himself,

These days are special. Your life has taken on a great purpose. Indulge yourself. Clean the living room. A time of such importance as this ought to be marked. The corridor from the bedroom to the dining room is not worthy of your enlarged spirit.

I flew from such a self-indulgence as this. There is great honor in labor, and greater honor in consistent labor. Despite my feeling that these days were special and magical, I kept on with my itinerary of domestic purgation.

I do not change clothes to clean, any more than I change clothes to cook. A man who is careful and methodical in such business will not soil himself. A man who has his wits about him can prepare himself an eight-course meal, consume it, and afterwards comb the dirt from a room-size carpet, all in evening dress. I condemn uniforms and aprons.

The corridor from the bedroom to the dining room is of medium length, with a door at either end opening onto the rooms in question, and a third door just about equidistant—ten centimeters nearer the dining room in point of fact—between them. This door opens onto a linen closet. It was just at the frame of this door that I had left off the night before.

First I oiled the hinges and polished them till they shone. Then, with a solution of ammonia and water, in a mixture precisely measured, I washed the frame of the door with a soft cloth. I stood on a step-ladder and with a second cloth I scrubbed away the grime that had accumulated at the top of the frame. I next washed the door itself, first working on the five rectangular panels inset into it, and then on the articulated mouldings around these insert panels, then on the door itself. I polished the crystal doorknob with a special cloth reserved for only that purpose.

I propped open the door and washed its vertical edge. I then scrubbed the top edge. With a cloth wrapped around the edge of a strong tongue of wood, I rubbed along the bottom edge of the door. (Once every other cleaning I remove the door from its hinges entirely and lay it down in the corridor, but this was the off-turn.)

I repeated, for the inside of the door, all that I had done for the outside. It might well be that I would not even open that door again until its time had come around again for cleaning, but I was not going to deny myself the satisfaction of knowing I had performed my task well.

In my vigorous scrubbing I happened to knock a chip of paint from the moulding of the second insert panel from the bottom on the inside of the door. I was not cast down by this accident as some men might have been. I was prepared. In the corridor that runs between the kitchen and the living room is another closet in which I keep cans of all the various paints with which the walls, ceilings, floors, and woodwork of the apartment are painted, each labeled clearly and succinctly. I went immediately to this closet, and on the fourth shelf—the shelf marked *Corridors*—I took the small can which read in neat lettering on a small gummed label:

BEDROOM—DINING ROOM
CLOSET DOOR
INTERIOR

I picked out a brush, and returned with the can, feeling a real satisfaction in my own care and forethought.

I touched up the chipped paint and returned the can to its proper place. I set a little oscillating fan in front of the open door to speed the drying. Meanwhile, I began work on the interior of the closet itself. Inside, from floor to ceiling are six compartments each with a brass latch, opening downwards. I rubbed all the wood—gumwood, I believe—with a pine-scented oil, employing three different cloths. I polished each of the brass latches until it shone. I opened each of the compartments and removed the few linens I had stored there, placing them along the length of the corridor in the precise ordering I had removed them. Then I polished the inside of each of the six compartments, drying them carefully so that none of the oil would penetrate the linens when I replaced them. This took some time since I was as careful with the first as with the last. That is my way.

From the top of the three drawers in the kitchen where I keep light bulbs, I took a newish one-hundred-fifty watt bulb, sprayed it with the ammonia solution, and carefully wiped it clean and dry. Then I unscrewed the bulb that was already in place at the top of the closet and replaced it with the bulb from the drawer. I readily admit that most men do not see the need of cleaning light bulbs, but I labor under a certain disability. I do not perceive colors as most men do. All the lights in my apartment are as bright as the fixtures will allow. They give off strong, perfectly white light. It is only in this manner that I am able to pick out colors at all. Even at one-hundred-fifty watts, I am at difficulty to distinguish red and purple, say, which to me appear no more than a gray faded from pink and a gray faded from lavender. I wash and polish the light bulbs not in hope that I will thereafter be able to distinguish colors, but only so that my meager skill in that direction may not be further diminished.

By the time I was done with that, the paint on the inside moulding of the door was dry. I didn't touch it—if I had left a fingerprint in it, I would have felt obligated to scrape it off and begin again. But I felt confident that the paint was indeed dry and rested satisfied with my own inward conviction. I tested the latch of each compartment and found each in working order. I carefully refolded all the linens and replaced them in the proper compartments. I removed the oscillating fan and returned it to its proper place in the closet off the corridor between the living room and the bathroom. Folding a new cloth over the crystal doorknob, I carefully shut the closet door, satisfied that I had accomplished my duty for the evening, despite my fevered brain, which reeled with the significance of its new-found purpose.

Annie's neighborhood is fashionable with a younger crowd. One rarely hears anything but English spoken there. Rents are high. Rapes are few. A shop specializing in spices is at the corner of Annie's block, and next to it a little restaurant with four or five tables on the sidewalk. I saw a number of persons sitting out in the warm evening, languidly stirring, with long spoons, tall glasses of iced chocolate.

Annie was one of them.

"I knew you'd come by here," she said.

I sat down beside her, and when the waiter came, I ordered iced chocolate as well. I'm not actually certain that the restaurant served anything else.

I did not ask Annie about her parents. I wasn't sure that I believed in them.

"I have some new pictures to show you," said Annie, meaningfully.

All Annie's molars were gold. They glinted in the moonlight.

"And I bought you a book today," she said. "On the way to the train station. When I took my mother."

The waitress came out with my chocolate.

"Where was your father?" I asked. "Didn't he go too?"

The persons at the next table rose and departed, having left the money for their bill and a tip on a small rectangular tray provided by the waitress.

"Oh," said Annie, "I thought I told you. They're getting a divorce."

"You did say that," I concurred. "Some time ago."

A derelict Negro lurched up the sidewalk, carrying a folded newspaper in his right hand. He wasn't so familiar a sight here as he would have been in my neighborhood. Annie stared at him. He caught her eye and stumbled. He just managed to steady himself against the table next to ours.

He righted himself and was about to walk on, but Annie looked up and said, "Excuse me, sir."

When he looked around, Annie deftly raised her arm high and brought it down against his folded newspaper. It fell out of his hand, and so did the tray and the cash he had secreted beneath it.

The Negro staggered off as Annie gathered up the bills and the change and replaced them on the table.

"Mommy's testifying that Daddy beat her," said Annie. "Once, she said, he nearly strangled her."

Annie stretched her legs in the warm spring moonlight. The stripes of her cotton trousers converged on her thin ankles. Her tiny, delicate feet were encased in polished white pumps with black silk bows.

Would I confide in her, I wondered? Would I tell her of my plan to help Marta to die?

10

When Annie and I had finished our chocolate we walked back toward her flat. I had already decided to tell her about Marta. Annie is a sensible girl, and she would have been convinced, immediately and with all the irrefutable force that had weighed me down in the beginning, that Marta must be helped to die.

Perhaps if I had spoken to Annie about it all, I wouldn't be writing this now.

No, that's wrong, when I think of all that came after.

At any rate, as we neared the stoop of Number TWENTY-NINE, I was on the very point of speaking, of opening my mouth and forming my words,

Yesterday, I needed a particular spice...

Yet I said nothing. My mouth clamped shut in surprise. I halted and stared down at the ground.

Annie stopped, too, and looked at me puzzled.

I hurried on, not wanting her—I'm not certain why—to see what I had seen.

On the sidewalk, carefully drawn in chalk, was a winged hourglass and the scrawled legend

TEMPUS FUGIT

I was disturbed to find the Fuggits' logo outside my own neighborhood, where gangs, after all, were not unknown. I was even more distressed to discover it so near Annie's flat. I remembered how surprised I was that Howard knew anything of them, that, indeed, my question regarding them had constituted the password that had opened Howard's mouth. Howard even knew their names: Shade and Shadow, Clay, Dust, and Ashes. I was uncomfortable to find that they had preceded me to this spot, that one of them, stooping with a stick of chalk, had drawn the sign and perhaps said to the others, *He'll know we were thinking of him.* Yet how had they known of my decision to visit Annie on this particular night? And who, for that matter, had informed them of Annie's existence and Annie's address?

For the moment, and merely because of the chalked scrawl, I said nothing to Annie about my plan.

Annie's building has a high stoop, but once inside the front doors, she has to descend two flights to her flat in the sub-basement. Her apartment is long and narrow, with a kitchen, a dining room, a bedroom, and a living room, arranged in a line from the front of the building to the back. However, because the whole apartment is quite below the level of the ground, she has but a single window, and that right up against the ceiling in her living room at the very back. The building furnace is just behind the wall of her bedroom, and when it is on, the apartment is stifling hot. The walls, plunged into the earth, sweat and bleed. Yet because of the fashionableness of the neighborhood, she pays more than I for this Tarturus of flats.

Her furniture was bought new and fashionably, but all the fabrics are stained from the hot damp, all the wood is warped from the cold dew. Even the glass coffee table seems to sweat. When the plaster sheered off the walls in great sheets, Annie left the walls bare stone and bare brick.

On the walls are large photographs made from negatives that have come through the machines in her shop. They are kept on the walls until discolored and rotten by the damp, then replaced with others. Annie examines every picture that comes in to her. The photographs in the living room are inoffensively pretty: pictures of mountain picnics, or of gulls and terns feeding on an empty beach, or of some frightened animal on the African veldt. Those in the bathroom are humorous: pouting infants, gambolling kittens, bewildered pedestrians. The photographs in the bedroom are shockingly rude.

Whenever I surreptitiously open drawers in Annie's flat, I always find stacks of photographic prints inside, neatly arranged and categorized, secured with elastic bands.

Up the stoop, down the hall, down the stairs, around the furnace, into Annie's flat.

"Here are your gifts," she said, picking them off a shaky table. The glue had melted away in the joints, leaving the legs rickety.

We sat down on the couch.

She gave me a book:

THINGS CALLED BY THEIR RIGHT NAME

"Did you read the one I gave you last week?" she asked. *"The Morals of Pleasure?"*

I kissed her and opened her blouse. "I threw it away."

She gave me two shirts, so highly colored that even I, with my impaired visual sense, could make out that one was red and one was yellow.

"Did you wear the shirts I gave you two weeks ago?" she asked, as I pressed the palms of my hands over her breasts. "The one that was blue and the one that was purple?"

"I used them as dust wipes," I replied.

She removed my hands and closed her blouse. We sat down on the couch. The furnace came on with a grating roar. The room was instantly suffused with heat. The brick walls began to bleed.

"Mommy brought me a photo album from my childhood," said Annie. "Let's look at it together."

The album was brand-new. It still bore the price sticker on the lower left-hand corner of the cover. Annie and I sat next to one another. I put my arm around her shoulder, and she opened the album across our laps.

"That's Mommy and Daddy before they were married," she said, pointing at the first picture. "He didn't beat her then."

The young man and woman in the photograph wore modern, faintly fashionable clothes. The photograph was obviously recent.

Annie turned the pages, pointing out and naming various members of her family and telling brief stories about each.

"That's Bobby, my only boy cousin. He used to show me his prick and make me touch it."

She continued to turn the pages. None of the persons in the album looked alike. All the photographs were very recent. Aunt Judy was a Negress. I did not let on to Annie that I knew she had taken photographs from her shop and pasted them in this album.

"Who is that?" I asked occasionally, pointing at a figure in one of the photographs.

"That is Sally," Annie would say. "Sally and I were best friends but she died in a car wreck."

Or I'd comment, "That man has a nose just like yours."

And Annie would say, "I'm not surprised. That's my grandfather. He lived to be ninety-eight, and then he was run over by a streetcar in Canada."

I'd seen other albums of Annie's, albums that purported to be of her high school friends or of her coworkers at the ribbon factory or of her father's French relatives. They were all the same: new albums with new photographic prints so recently pasted in that the glue was still tacky in places. One she showed me over and over again was the album of her baby pictures, but these photographs were so evidently of scores of different infants in as many different houses and flats and locales that I found it impossible to maintain even a remote belief in them.

I do not pry into Annie's life. That would be inconsistent with the perfect trust I repose in her. I am not the one to point out that what Annie represents as her immediate family and the entire of her past is no more than a miscellany of photographs taken by city office workers and compiled by her very nearly at random.

I see Annie's transparent subterfuge here not as, say, an orphan's pitiable attempt to construct a family and a personal history. I see it rather as a charming prelude to sex, all the more titillating for its very innocuousness.

Annie and I never have sex without looking through an album first.

I've no need to urge my penis *up* when one of those albums is opened across her lap and mine. It knows what is to follow.

"Want to see another?" Annie always asks after the last picture of Uncle Bill posing on the walls of Masada.

"Yes," I reply invariably, and out comes another album.

I smoothly flatten my lap as this second album is opened.

The photographs here are of a different nature altogether. They, too, are taken from her customers' rolls of film. Annie enlarges them in a room at the back of the shop, on her lunch break.

We rarely comment on these photographs, which Annie invariably produces—for my sake—in black-and-white, though the originals may have been in color.

Annie, however, may remark, "This one is new. It came in yesterday."

We note with little slips of paper those we are most intrigued by, and when we've gone through the album completely we return to these.

Annie's blouse is open again.

I do not bother to flatten my lap.

Annie much prefers her work in the photographic shop to her former employment at the ribbon factory.

Annie and I have a single bone of contention. She would like to emulate some of the photographs. I on the other hand prefer to employ the second album of photographs only as a means to arousal. I find the photographs, in point of fact, disgusting.

My preference prevails, of course.

I don't do variations.

A man who is sure of himself performs the sexual act in the prescribed fashion.

Variations are made up by women who have not been satisfied in bed. Men would never have thought of them on their own.

Variations are indulged in only by those men who are uncertain of their masculinity. They are men with withered scrotums. Or, worse, they are at base homosexuals.

Annie and I peruse these photographs at our leisure. The furnace knocks and cracks and bellows. The stone walls sweat and the brick walls bleed.

I insist that Annie remove all her clothing. All her jewelry. She scrubs the lipstick and eyeshadow from her face. She stands in the shower and the powder and dry deodorant run from her body and spiral down the drain. I insist that she be naked. Even the sight of her gold molars is distressing to me. They seem to me a kind of jewelry. I asked once if she'd have them removed, and this was the only thing Annie ever refused me.

It was an unsettled question in my mind whether Annie fucked any man but me. Certainly I was faithful to her. So far as I was concerned our relationship was perfect. Annie was my sister. I memorized her body. I loved every part of it but her gold molars. They always came as a surprise. It was a possibility, however, that Annie herself did not consider our relationship perfect. I know that women's desires are different from men's. Women also, for that matter, have no working concept of perfection. Incapable of it, they are also incapable of recognizing it. It was only logical, therefore, that Annie would *not* think our relationship all it might have been.

Her desire for variations alone showed that, I suppose.

I was not bothered by Annie's blindness to the perfection of our relationship. She wasn't *capable* of recognizing it; therefore I did not blame her for her shortcoming. I only wondered if her perceived but unjustified discontent was so strong that she was driven into the embrace of any man other than myself. It was a possibility. I saw Annie generally no more than once a week. She had opportunity. She might even receive propositions behind her counter. A man who had brought in rude negatives, receiving them as developed prints, might remark with a leer, "Did you look through these?"

Annie wouldn't be the woman to deny she had, if that were the case. It would be the case, for Annie looked at all her photographs.

"Yes," Annie would say.

"Did you like what you saw?" the man would ask.

"It's no more than I've seen and done in the flesh," I can imagine Annie saying.

Things would go from there, on evenings when I did not see her.

These men, if they existed in Annie's life, did not satisfy her. If they had satisfied her, she would never have thought of variations. It was their inadequacy—if they existed—that drove Annie to beg me to swerve from my invariable course. I did not blame these men, but I despised their shrivelled sacs and their hidden burning desires.

I was not jealous. Jealousy never entered my brain within those sweating, bleeding walls of Annie's flat. The hammering that beat in my head was no more than the expansion and contraction of the walls of the ancient furnace. The mere unflawed roundness of my being precluded jealousy of the inadequate.

Yet I wondered.

Inside of Annie, my penis was whitely sheathed in the coagulating pools of other men's unfertile slime.

When Annie opened her mouth, I saw the reflection of their straining faces, at the riotous moment of expulsion, shining on the corrugated surface of her golden molars.

On four golden molars shone the faces of four different spindling men, aroused by Annie's cactus beauty. They spewed their slime in decadent variations contrived by generations of the race of unsatisfied human females.

I examined Annie's body under a lamp. Splotches of shiny skin denoted old pools of slime, shot out upon her variously, allowed to dry, and finally rubbed into the epidermis.

I climbed atop her, entered her, thrust, and emptied my testicles of their most potent white mead.

The brick walls bled, but Annie evidently hadn't.

She intimated that she might be with child.

She took the album with photographs of babies out from under the bed and leafed through it.

"My baby will look like that," she said, pointing at one of the infants no more hideous than the others.

I said nothing.

There are ways and means of dealing with infants. Children are conceived of whom no photograph is ever taken. I've seen brass plates on out-of-the-way doors that suggest solutions within. I spoke vaguely of all this.

Annie, if she understood, pretended not to.

She went into the bathroom and shut the door behind her. The knocking of the furnace all but covered the noise of running water. I stood out of the bed and pressed my brow against the sweating stone wall of Annie's bedroom.

When Annie came out of the bathroom, I went in, shut the door, and vomited into the toilet.

Rising to my feet a few moments later, I upset a bottle of prescribed medicine on the lid of the toilet. Without thought I picked it up and read the label. The name of the medication—a pale separated liquid—meant nothing to me, but I noted with alarm that it had come from the pharmacy that employed Howard Dormin. Howard himself, perhaps, had brought the bottle to Annie's door.

Howard, I may have said, I do not class as an ordinary young man.

I can conceive, for instance, that his loins might provide issue.

Annie's child, if there was one lodged in her womb, might be Howard's.

Howard had come far afield to this neighborhood, it was true. He may have been winded climbing Annie's steep stoop. He may have had difficulty in finding his way down the darkened hallway to the narrow door that led down, down to Annie's subterranean flat. He may even have stumbled on the stairs, nearly smashing the bottle of liquid medication. It would have shook in his grasp, its separated layers mixing again. He would have knocked on the door, wondering if his summons could be heard over the noise of the furnace, bleating and striking like the furnaces of Hell, and he may have been kept waiting by Annie, who did not know him. But all this trouble would have proved no trouble at all, for Annie threw wide the door, opened her blouse, raised her skirt, and drew Howard to her. She claimed no variation, and the bottle of medicine was held locked in their clasped sweating hands.

If there was a child, then it was Howard who should provide and not I.

Of all this, I said nothing to Annie when I emerged from the bathroom. She lay asleep, her invaded belly exposed.

The album of infants lay open on the floor next to the bed. I softly closed it. I went into the living room and took my sleeping blinders from the inside breast pocket of Suit S-6. The left-hand patch is black, and the right-hand patch is white. I put them on, lay down upon the couch and slept the sleep of the righteous.

I awoke at dawn. The sun shone through the single small window high up in the wall. On the screen covering the window, in white chalk, was drawn the figure of the winged hourglass. Its black webbed shadow fell cool upon my face.

I left the apartment without telling Annie what the future held for Marta and myself.

II

I told Howard Dormin the truth when I mentioned that I work on Saturday. I would not have said so if my Employer had been present, for my Employer does not know that I appear in the office on that sixth day.

Saturday, in fact, is my favorite day for work, for a number of reasons.

The first is that there isn't anything I must accomplish. My Employer, not knowing I come in on that day, has left no tasks for me on the red deal table between our offices.

The second is that the building is otherwise empty. On Saturday I do not even hear the surreptitious footpads in the loft above.

The street outside is deserted and clear of trash.

Across the way, the city offices of employment, or unemployment, are closed and unlighted.

I sit alone at my desk. I count my Employer's pencils at my leisure. I watch Karl out of the windows at the back of the loft. This neighborhood, made of light manufacturing concerns and small offices, has very few residents. Most of these last are illegal tenants I suspect, squatters perhaps or renters despite zoning restrictions. I conjecture that Karl must feel very much alone on Saturdays and Sundays.

He rises late on Saturday. His coffee pot is of tin or perhaps aluminum.

I stood at the back window and waited for Karl to show himself at his window. On some Saturdays he does not appear before eleven in the morning, or even noon. I am patient, however, for I've nothing else to do in the office.

This particular Saturday, in Suit S-1, my oldest and most comfortable, I leaned against the corner of my Employer's desk, patiently watching for Karl's appearance and piecing together all that had happened in the past two days.

This was a task of some complexity and import.

I first reviewed all that had occurred in the Baltyk Kitchen, shuddering just to recall my first glimpse of Marta. I brought to mind all that she had said, that I had said, that I had heard said about her. I visualized her apartment building, Number NINETY-FOUR.

I retraced the reasoning that had led me inescapably to the conclusion that Marta wanted to die and that I of all men on Earth must assist her, for both our sakes, equally.

I found no fault in that reasoning. I had not expected to.

This review was only a self-indulgent prelude to my real concern that Saturday morning, and that was the business of what had followed.

Three things of importance had occurred after Marta's lifeline crossed mine.

I had seen, for the first time, the gang whose insignia was a winged hourglass. Moreover, this gang in some vague but pronounced manner, seemed cozily cognizant of my existence.

Second, Howard Dormin—a young man I have seen about for more than a year—suddenly took on a different character. He was revealed to be a Messenger. He also, it turned out, knew about the gang and provided me with their collective name—the Fuggits, and their individual names—Shade and Shadow for the two women, Clay, Dust, and Ashes for the three indistinguishable young men.

Third, Annie intimated to me that she might be pregnant. And I discovered that there was some, albeit possibly slight or even unconscious, connection between Annie and Howard, and Annie and the gang. A bottle of medicine in Annie's subterranean flat was procured at the pharmacy that employs Howard. (It was even possible that Howard was the father of the child whose existence Annie seemed anxious to credit to the potency of the slime in my testicles.) The Fuggits scrawled their sign on the sidewalk outside Annie's building and on the screen of the single window of Annie's flat.

Now it was possible, certainly, that all this circumstance was innocent, or indeed, occurred only in my mind, fevered with the thought of my newfound purpose. On the other hand, it was just possible that the links between Annie and Howard, between Annie and the Fuggits, between Howard and the Fuggits, were real, strong-forged, and purposeful.

And if the latter, what was their purpose?

I could scarcely believe that it had nothing to do with Marta.

It was possible I was being led a merry chase. The death of Marta was a part of a larger plan coined in the brain of Another. I was the mere instrument. It was the job of the Fuggits, Annie, and Howard to make certain I fulfilled this duty.

I did not like the feeling that I was chained to Another's purpose. For the first time, I wondered if Marta and her longed-for death were not mere aberrations of my brain, implanted by Another. Perhaps even her supreme hideousness existed only in the shard of command that had been implanted in my head.

I could not, I decided, kill merely at the behest of Another.

My mind, in these ruminations, had been drawn away from the buildings across the courtyard. Some movement in one of the windows drew my eye, and I refocused my attention.

Two of the windows—somewhat to the right of those in which I was accustomed to seeing Karl—were lighted from within. The day was heavily overcast, yet still the lights must have been very bright in those rooms for me to have seen into them as clearly as I did. I even seemed to remember that before, I had seen those windows blocked by stacks of cartons.

But here was an apartment, with a palm in the corner and framed photographs on the white walls and a door with chains.

I raised my binoculars to my eyes.

The chains on the door were undone. I could even detect a slight motion in them, as if they had only that moment been released. The door swung open, and a figure stepped resolutely into the room.

My mind was about to identify that figure. I know it was. But then the light went out. I could no longer see inside the apartment. The windows were dark and blank. I thought I could even make out stacks of cartons where before there had been a palm on a polished wooden floor. My mind had been about to say, *That figure is no other than Howard Dormin.*

I sometimes am a step or two ahead of my mind. Not infrequently I can predict what my mind will think, conjecture, conclude. This was one of those times. If the lights in that apartment had remained on one-tenth of one second longer, my mind would have told me, *Howard Dormin is there.*

I put down my binoculars and counted the number of windows I could see from the vantage of my Employer's desk. On six different buildings, I made out forty-seven windows.

All of them were dark. Their panes were black and unreflecting.

In a systematic pattern, I trained my field glasses on the windows of each building, beginning at my far left and proceeding to my right.

Nothing, nothing, black panes, and at most a glimpse of boards or boxes piled or stacked just behind the windows. Some of the windows were of frosted glass or had been painted white.

From ONE to FORTY-SEVEN I had seen nothing. I put down my binoculars and rubbed my weary eyes.

Suddenly something was flung from one of those windows. It was dark and squarish, but I couldn't make it out exactly. It arced in the air for a moment, then plummeted to the courtyard below with a crash.

I raised my glasses and peered through them across the courtyard. The FORTY-SEVEN windows were black and empty.

I stood and watched for half an hour longer. No lights came on. I detected no movement but that of Karl, who appeared at last at his accustomed window and filled his tin, or aluminum, coffee pot at the tap.

In order to rest my eyes, I walked to the front of the loft and looked out those windows for a while.

The six alcoholics who inhabit the abandoned car in front of the building are unmolested by me on Saturday. Three of them sat in the vehicle today. One of the back wheels had been taken off during the night. To maintain balance the men had propped the car on cement blocks. They tossed an empty bottle from one of the windows and it smashed in the middle of the street.

I sat down at my desk and found that I was listening, with some trepidation, for the sound of the elevator starting up.

I was fearful, I discovered, that the Fuggits had followed me to this place. If Howard were across the courtyard, then the gang might well be downstairs. Howard and the Fuggits might even be in communication, with the aid and apparatus of synchronized timepieces and short-wave telephones.

Here, on Saturday, I was alone.

If I were attacked, the drunks in the abandoned car would not come to my aid. They knew it was I who telephoned the police against them every weekday.

I was pleased to reflect that the elevator operated only with the use of a key. Therefore I was safe so long as I remained in my Employer's loft.

But what would happen when I decided that it was time to return home? There was the possibility that the five members of the gang had crowded into the tiny entrance of the building, waiting for me to appear at the end of my sixth work day. I would be attacked as I left the elevator. I fancied the sensation of my cheeks pressed against the grimy linoleum. I seemed to hear the cracking of the bones of my right arm.

I leaned out one of the front windows and gazed down the front of the building for several minutes. I could detect no movement there. When the drunks caught sight of me and began yelling imprecations, I withdrew. On a sheet of stationery bearing my Employer's name I drew an hourglass and attached wings to it. I taped it to the window directly behind my chair.

I remained uneasy. I decided to go home early. This was not my custom, but then, none of my days recently had gone according to form. And anyway, who was to stop me? My Employer did not even know I was there, and had he known, he might even have objected.

I returned to his office just to make certain that everything was in its place. It would not do to have traces of my sixth day occupancy.

Almost against my will, I glanced out again at the array of buildings behind. At first I was relieved to find all of the windows black, dark, and empty.

Only Karl was there, standing with his back to the windows, in his white kimono shot with large black ideographs. He held his tin coffee pot aloft. He turned his head and leered at me over his shoulder, the way crowds at Tyburn leered at the neck-doomed.

I walked home, giving not a thought to the possibility that I would be waylaid by the Fuggits.

I did not even remonstrate when the alcoholics in the abandoned automobile flung a bottle at my head.

My resolve was shaken.

I worried, as I said, that the oath to help Marta to die was an alien implant in my brain.

My soul's vow was no more than a metal chip engraved with a cold command.

Howard, Annie, and the gang were all part of the business.

I was undecided what I should do.

I went into the long hallway between my living room and my bathroom, and let the door swing shut. I sat down with my back against the closet door there and, in the dark, pondered what ought to be my course.

It seemed impossible to think ahead. There was too much I did not know.

The connections between Howard, Annie, and the gang might, after all, exist only in my mind.

I'd keep my appointment with Howard. It was possible that Howard would make all things clear.

I had several hours to pass before I was to see him.

I continued to ponder the events of the past few days. I began with the wanting spice and the sign upon the grocery door. I ended with myself, slumped against the closet door in the darkened hallway.

It all came down to Marta.

She was the kernel.

Everything proceeded from her.

Only by returning to her would things be made clear again in my soul.

It was possible that an attempt was being made to control me from without. Such things happen with a frequency undreamt of in most men's minds. I did not finally doubt, however, my ability to withstand such external manipulation. When I saw Marta again, I would know whether my vow were soul-forged or no.

There was a bond between us, our antipodean essences.

No one could come between us.

I was nervous. I did not like to consider these contingencies or to imagine there was some connection between all these persons who touched my life.

While waiting for the time to go to Howard's, I might have cleaned my apartment. Yet my concentration wasn't what it should be for that task.

I decided I would make an effort to clear my brain and cleanse my soul.

I stripped and put on fresh underwear. I went into the living room and seated myself on the sofa facing my self-portrait and took up my sketchbook.

I am a splendid draftsman. I do not count that talent as part of my superiority. A man, theoretically, may be whole as a human being, but lack any particular talent as an artist, say, or as a mathematical theoretician. My skill with a pen is *on top of* my basic perfection. The gravy, Annie would say, on the icing. My self-portrait is a truer image of me than anything I have ever seen thrown back at me from a mirror. A mirror shows me a fleeting image of my essence, but at one isolated moment in eternity; the self-portrait, on the other hand, is not rooted in a particular moment. It is timeless. Anyone looking at my self-portrait would instantly say:

Ah, there is a man born to perfection, who is now—as it were—at the peak of perfection. Here is a man who will sigh away perfection with his dying breath.

I draw one picture a night, and that picture is the theme—as it were—of my masturbation.

I never know what I will draw. Each night's work is different. I have volumes of these drawings, and oddly enough, each drawing has power over my libidinousness for that one night alone. Then it is novel and almost harrowing in its ability to arouse me. It has, in its freshness, more reality than real life itself can show. After it has served its purpose, however, it is stale, flat, and lifeless, and no more to be regarded than a billboard advertisement for something I've no interest at all in obtaining.

Only occasionally do I even glance through the volumes and volumes of drawings I have done, and then it is only out of a cold curiosity to determine some pattern in my unconsciousness. I've never made out that pattern. The sequence of drawings seems random. All are finely wrought, of course, but it's as if they had been done by as many different artists as there are drawings. These pictures, however, are primarily a means of nocturnal release and only incidentally a matter for even superficial personal investigation. As I draft, I do not trouble myself with what has come before and what may come after. I am wholly involved with the present page. I think of nothing else.

As I took up my pen, I wondered briefly.

Will this drawing be more than the others?

By more, I meant, would it partake of the specialness of the night itself?

How would that new beginning affect this drawing?

I thought no more about it. The pen took on a life of its own. I did not attempt to dissuade it from any particular stroke it wished to make.

My pen drew the curve of a muscular shoulder and arm.

I was not surprised at this. Sometimes my pen begins with the man—as did Life itself—and only afterwards is the woman added.

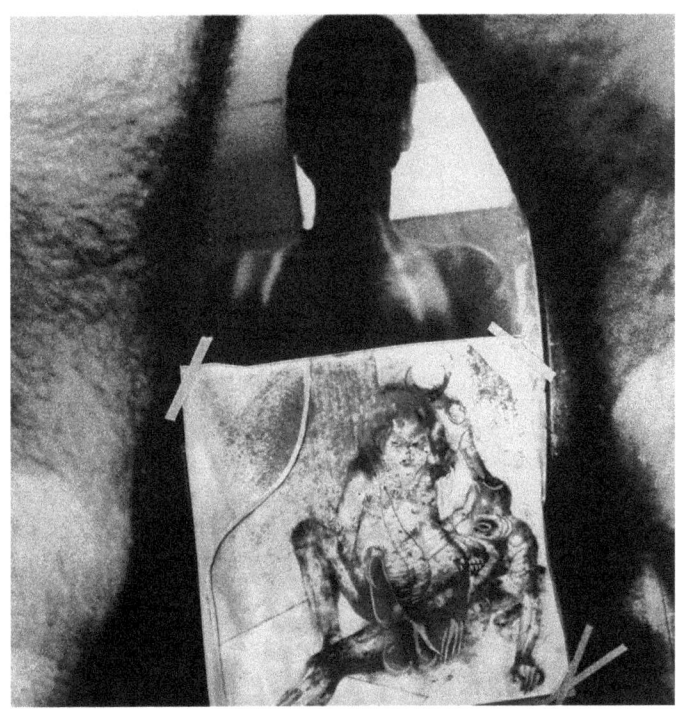

Will this drawing be more than the others?

My pen, in light strokes, continued with the masculine figure. It laid him out on the floor, in the corner of an empty room. Shoulders pulled off the floor, head thrown back and featureless, one leg stretched out, the other bent sharply at the knee. A man, no more and no less, rising from a heavy sleep he did not remember having entered.

The picture was different from any I had ever drawn, yet somehow it wasn't an unexpected image. I thoughtlessly reflected a little disappointment, impatient with the drawing that was presenting itself to my perusal.

With only a masculine figure before me, of course, my pen wasn't done. Not even when it had drawn in the exposed sex of the man, dragging scrotum, high curving penis. I waited. Nothing more. My own sex stirred irresolutely, in futile search of prey that had been promised.

My pen rose straight and then dropped down onto the paper. I awaited the outcome with curiosity and—I confess it—some alarm. Against accident, my left hand was thrust up under the hem band of my underpants.

A pair of female buttocks planted themselves across the torso of the supine man. This was promising. I admired the effect. The satyrical penis now arched up toward the body that would doubtless be filled and filled in.

I breathed relief. I had drawn, I saw now, merely another brothel tableau. A gentleman of demented imagination has purchased the services of a whore, to sit upon his belly, to squeeze his internal organs till passion rose. It is the end of a long damp night. A sullen dawn glows glumly behind thick draperies my pen had seen no need to delineate. These two alone, old acquaintances perhaps, perhaps not, feast alone in the top-most room of the house of ill-fame. There is something elemental in this man's warped passion, for at base—my brain informed me—all passion is base. The more strangled and engorged and squeezed a passion, the nearer it is to its essential self.

I thought:

I'll finish the woman, sitting upon the man's belly, study the picture for a few moments, imagining other details, and afterwards, make quick work of it.

I believe in masturbation. No man should go to sleep with his testicles full of slime. In sleep, the slime seeps into the blood and pollutes the hidden corners of the body. Masturbation is a salutary, even necessary cleansing rite.

I waited, a little impatiently, for my pen to finish the figure. Truth to tell, I was suddenly weary and seemed like to fall asleep. I believe I even closed my eyes for a few moments, trusting that when I opened them again, the second figure would be completed. It hadn't to be a finished portrait of the whore after all. I was only seeing her from the back, and I had formulated the principal limits of the story already. A few quick strokes of the pen, and then a few quick strokes more, and I'd be done. I even willed my penis up, in expectation of a prompt release.

I opened my eyes and was revulsed.

The second figure had been completed, but not in any manner

I could have predicted and certainly not in a manner that was conducive to my limited purpose.

The buttocks of the woman were no longer buttocks. They were her immense dragging breasts. The completed figure was perched harpylike atop the man's torso, serene, malevolent, disinterested. One clawed hand was reaching slowly toward his scrotum. Her skin was a waste of contagion, moled and suppurated.

Then I saw something worse—that perhaps the buttocks that were breasts were not breasts at all, but merely an enlarged scrotum, engorged with slime. A detached scrotum with a woman's dreadful head sewn atop it, a waddling, slopping monstrosity.

My pen wasn't done. It drew the beginnings of a frightful face upon the torso of the man who struggled beneath this enlarged, feminized scrotum. It drew another curving penis protruding from his forehead and a sac that spilled down the contour of his neck, so that yet the contents of a third scrotum rolled upon his chest.

I studied the figures, and then I stared at my hand that held the pen, almost with the thought that it had betrayed me.

My penis remained up, pressing against the fabric of my undershorts, uselessly. This picture would not serve. I willed it down.

I put the pen aside. At the cost of destroying the perfection of the album, I ripped the stiff page free—the first time I had ever taken such a step—and took it to the mantel where I propped it against the mirror. For a few minutes I alternately stared at it and at my pained, perplexed reflection.

It occurred to me suddenly that before I had placed the pen in my hand, I had wondered,

Will this drawing be more than the others?

That was the answer. This picture *was* different and more. It was somehow commensurate with the change in my life.

I stared at the second figure more carefully now, to see if I could interpret it. All violent anomalies have meaning.

It is Marta there.

I seemed to hear the words spoken in the room. Yet I did not speak them, and no one else was there.

That didn't matter, however. What mattered was that I had drawn a picture of Marta—or rather, Marta's essence, her soul. She was an illogical, unparalleled, inescapable presence.

For a few moments I fretted that she had spilled out of the pen reserved for the delineation of my masturbatory fantasies. Was there, irreconcilable as the thought might be, somewhere deep inside me an attraction to this aberrant changeling, this earth-bound moon-calf?

No, I decided as I returned to the couch with the page, that could not be. This figure I had drawn was merely the antithesis of all that was desirable. Marta's very existence argued an antipodal and perfected paradigm of beauty. She was the precise negative of the ultimate phantasm of desire.

Staring at Marta's soul, I pushed down the front of my underpants. Without my command and certainly without my willing it, the slime of my testicles gushed across the drawing.

12

I was unnerved by the thought that Marta might have slipped into my masturbatory fantasies. I imagined her having held her hand briefly over my head in the Baltyk. A single drop of her blood had dropped from a single finger onto my head. It had burned through hair and scalp and settled on my white skull. It had softened it, and she seeped through into my brain. That single drop of acid had invaded my head, and the image of Marta had established itself as a Venusian goddess who raised the sluice-gates of my slime.

I had thought of her too much, I decided.

I had scarcely thought of anything else was the fact.

Was my memory of her perfect?

Had I enlarged her? Had I shored up the statistics of her being? Was she as black as I had painted her—the very midnight of humanity?

It was necessary that I re-establish her in my brain, without prejudice, unaffected this time by the shock of seeing her without forewarning.

I'd be a very Perseus and walk upright into the bone-strewn temple.

I changed into Suit S-5. I left the apartment and went directly to the Baltyk Kitchen.

The afternoon was warm. Many people were on the street. Light streamed through the faded red curtains of the restaurant. The Baltyk Kitchen served food at all hours, but it had, I suppose, its slack times. This was one. Two old women were devouring a vast meal in one of the booths. Two old men sat at the bar with empty shot glasses before them. Now and then one of them pressed the glass to his mouth and darted his tongue inside, to lap up the film of liquor that remained.

The waitress was not Marta.

I sat at the bar, and pointed at the special on the chalkboard raised overhead.

The waitress gabbled at me in some unrecognizable tongue, then gabbled again, more loudly though, through the curtain into the kitchen.

I was disappointed not to see Marta but tried not to show it.

I was seized with panic the next instant when it occurred to me suddenly that Marta might already be dead. Having waited in vain for me to act, she had taken her own life. I saw her blood boiling up out of her slashed veins.

I recovered myself before anyone saw the horror in my eyes. Marta, I told myself, had never been possessed of the courage to kill herself. If she had possessed it, ever, she would never have hesitated a moment to tighten the noose. Marta, I was convinced, was still alive. I did not fear accidental death either. The mistake that brought her into the world was entrenched.

I sipped my water and recovered my equanimity.

An elderly, thin Negress came into the restaurant. In one hand she held an attaché case emblazoned with flags, and with the other hand she was holding up to her neck a rectangle of cardboard, which appeared to be fastened around her head with twine. She seated herself sidewise in one of the booths and, looking around the room sharply, caught my eye. She held it. She let the rectangle of cardboard fall. It was a collapsible sandwich board, neatly printed in capital letters in red and black.

I recovered myself before anyone saw the horror in my eyes.

The Negress smiled at me as I read:

>SUCKING FAGGOT VOTE IN THE
>SEVEN BOROUGHS M.F. SEX
>FIEND GOVERNOR OF THIS
>COUNTRY CITY STATE TOWN IS
>KILLING MY DAUGHTER MRS
>J C HODGES 94 HODGES
>STREET APARTMENT NUMBER
>ONE SEVEN *IN HER BATHTUB*
>GOD *MOTHER NATURE* STOP
>THESE COCK AND CUNT
>SUCKERS *ALMIGHTY GOD* HAS
>WRITTEN THAT COCK SUCKERS
>NEED TO KILL *BLACK NIGGERS*
>BEFORE THEY CAN KUM

"This government," she said loudly to the room in general, "is run by faggot priests and lesbian nuns."

The waitress brought her a glass of water and a menu.

The Negress opened the menu and unhesitatingly pointed out three items. The waitress closed the menu and took it away.

"Do you know," the Negress asked me loudly, "what is ruining this country?"

I said nothing.

She opened her briefcase. "Pornography!" she shouted. She withdrew two glossy magazines, slipped a finger into each and held them up high. Two over-long pages unfolded themselves to reveal, in her left hand, two men performing a grotesque and repellant sexual act, and on the right, a woman in carnal connection with a large black dog.

The Negress stood up and, with a stern pout on her face, showed the pictures to the two old women in the booth directly behind her. They averted their faces but said nothing.

The Negress walked all the way around the Baltyk Kitchen, holding the two magazines at arm's length before her, like obscene banners. She went back to her booth, carefully refolded the photographs, and placed the magazines back into her attaché case. She closed the case and locked it. She folded and hooked her sandwich board but left it around her neck like a wooden bib.

She slipped along the banquette and turned sideways so that she was facing out toward me.

"Do you know what's driving this country into the dirt?" she asked me in a loud whisper.

"No," I returned. "I've no idea."

She pointed lewdly at her own crotch, laughed, and slipped back into the booth. She said not another word all the time I was there and ate her food even demurely.

My food was brought. I smiled at the waitress and did not hesitate to eat what she had placed before me. It was a bowl of dark stew, containing beef, potatoes, carrots, leeks, and I know not what all else.

I had placed myself so that I might see the door to the street. I gazed continually at that entrance, at once hoping for and dreading Marta's appearance. Marta did not come.

I lingered over the last bit of stew and at last pushed my plate aside.

I ordered strudel again, and it was brought me.

I finished that, and still Marta did not come.

In that time, the two old women had got up and left. The old men had each gotten up twice and entered the lavatory. The old Negress departed with her sandwich board and attaché case. A young man and his girl had come in, ordered, eaten, paid, and left. Other diners had come in and were ordering.

Coffee was brought me. I let the cup sit in the saucer. I didn't relish it, had no intention of drinking it, but wanted to wait for Marta.

Marta did not come.

It was time for me to leave so that I might reach Howard's at the appropriate hour. I do not take any form of public transportation and haven't since my brother's accident. I walk everywhere.

The waitress brought my bill. I paid for it, stood up, and placing a generous tip in her hand, asked casually but distinctly, "Where is Marta this evening?"

The waitress dropped the change into the pocket of her apron. She replied with a smile: "Marta is in the kitchen."

She took up my untouched coffee. The cup slid awry in the saucer. Underneath, Marta's blood boiled up with a noisome hiss.

As I staggered out of the restaurant, I glanced toward the curtain that covered the entrance to the kitchen. It twitched. Marta was behind there.

I left, not having seen her, but inwardly convinced of the rightness of my vow. All the others—Annie, Howard, the gang, the guardians, the vagrants who accosted me on the street—were cardboard foils. It was Marta alone who mattered. Perhaps Another was indeed trying to persuade me to kill her. That was a possibility, but it did not concern me. It was a superfluous coincidence. I alone was concerned in this. For her sake and mine alone, it had to be done. The pact was between the two of us. No one else entered into it.

13

So much was clear: I didn't trust Howard Dormin. I'd hear what he had to say. I'd attend to his messages. I'd smile as he poured out his calculated confidences. But my mind was made up: Marta would die when and where and how it suited me.

I would use Howard as Howard was attempting to use me.

I followed the map that Howard left me. His neighborhood is nearby, contiguous to my own to the northeast. It is made up principally of red brick apartment buildings, constructed at the turn of the last century. I found Howard's house without difficulty.

The building was an anomaly: a square frame house, half a century earlier in date than the vast apartment houses that hemmed it in on three sides. Perhaps in that earlier time it had actually been a farm house, but its sloping meadows were now leveled concrete, its barns and sheds were crowded tenements, and its purling streams were black gutters brackish with the city's tears. The house was of four stories, with a crumbling verandah. Its yellow paint was soot-stained, faded, and peeling. It was a sad frail house in a sturdy anonymous neighborhood. I took an instant and instinctive dislike to it.

The wooden steps sagged as I mounted them.

The trousers of Suit S-5 were ripped as I tripped over the barbed wire strung at the top. I had not seen it in the fading afternoon light.

I twisted the bell and knocked loudly for good measure.

Howard appeared at the door, holding a bottle of medicine —as if the verandah were my flat, and *he* had rung to make a delivery. He invited me inside, and I went inside.

The hallway was wide and long, darkly papered, darkly carpeted, its length and breadth so crammed with furniture that we had to make several small turnings to get to the living room. I didn't know why Howard took me there as it too was so filled with furniture that it was scarcely maneuverable, and all the chairs and sofas were stacked high with books or cartons or piles of linen. The lights wouldn't work when Howard politely attempted to turn them on.

On the far side of the room, on the carved marble mantel of the hearth, was a gilded French clock, resolutely ticking away the final hours of Marta's unhappy life.

The ostensible reason of my visit was to meet Howard's grandfather. I saw no sign of the old man. In fact, I saw no sign of the house's being anything but a vast lumber room of dereliction.

Howard said, "Let's go up to the top."

I followed him up. The staircase was thickly carpeted so that our steps were muffled. Balusters were loose or broken or missing altogether. As we passed the second floor, I glanced down the hallway. The window at the end was shuttered and curtained. I detected a slight scrabbling, very likely a rat frightened by our presence. I had no conviction that Howard lived in this place.

We passed the third floor. That hallway was the same except that the window at the end of it was unshuttered and uncurtained. The panes were so grimy with dirt, however, that very little of the twilight penetrated.

We climbed to the top. Here were but two rooms, dormered, connected by a wide double door. They were, in sharp contrast to the rest of the house, very brightly lighted and empty.

In the first room were six full-sized cardboard cutouts of women, ectomorphs and endomorphs only. Their faces bore no features but for wide leering mouths painted in red lipstick, so thickly and recently applied I could smell it from across the room. Also, along one wall were stacked cages containing small live animals: rabbits in all the cages at the bottom of the wired pyramid, squirrels in the second tier, and rats crowded into the few cages along the top. All the animals, it seemed to me, were frightened. They scrabbled and chattered, thumped and mewed, twisted and hissed.

In the other room were two wooden crates and a handsomely carved glass-fronted cabinet. In the crates was ammunition, and guns filled the cabinet.

"My shooting gallery," said Howard with pride.

I looked about idly for a moment, and then Howard began to

show me his weapons, one by one, and talked of them in detail. He took from the cabinet revolvers and explained to me how they were loaded. He demonstrated how to hold a rifle so as not to be overturned by the recoil. He dropped boxes of ammunition into my hands to establish their surprising weight. We went into the other room and Howard exhibited his animals. He teased them with straws. He told me their names.

"What do you do with them?" I asked.

Howard grinned. He lifted one of the cages with the rats—there were five inside—and set it on the floor.

I retreated through the double doors into the other room. Howard raised the door of the cage. When he backed away, one by one the rats sniffed the air, ventured out, and then fled for cover.

In the empty room, however, there was no cover.

The rats cowered in the darkest corners, and they sidled along the cages of the rabbits. Howard stood laughing in the doorway. He took a pistol from his pocket and fired it five times. The shots were loud and echoing. I placed my hands over my ears. One by one, in astonishingly quick succession, the rats jumped up into the air, quivering and cartwheeling. Then, pausing in midair to exhale their depraved rodent souls in minute puffs of oily smoke, they dropped dead onto the floorboards.

The squirrels raced madly in their cages, the rabbits stood stock still and wept. Blood seeped out of the dead rats' bodies. There were other stains on the floor, I noted.

"You're lucky to have a girl," said Howard. He placed the barrel of the pistol to my nose and let me smell the burnt powder. I smiled faintly. The odor pleased me.

It took me a moment to realize he spoke of Annie and not of Marta.

"Annie thinks you're good-looking," I said in reply, making certain that the distinction was clear in *his* mind as well.

"What does she know?" said Howard contemptuously. "She's just a girl."

He turned smoothly and fired off the sixth bullet in the pistol. He caught one of the cardboard targets between its painted lips. Its shape was Marta's.

"You're lucky," he said, "because you don't have to pull your thing on the bathroom floor like a faggot."

He handed me the pistol.

"Which sort of bullets does this one use?" I asked curiously.

He went to the larger wooden crate, extracted a box of bullets, and showed me how it was loaded.

"See?" he said.

I nodded.

He took up one of several brown paper bags stored along the side of the crate of ammunition and went into the other room. He lifted the dead rats by their tails and dropped them inside.

He took his handkerchief out of his pocket and dropped it on the floor. Still carrying the brown paper bag in his crossed arms, he wiped up the blood using the toe of his boot as a propellant.

"I'll be back," he said, and disappeared down the stairs with the dead rats.

I was meant to take the pistol. That much was clear.

I put the gun into my pocket, then thought better of it. I took the gun out of my pocket, laid it on the floor, and then kicked it beneath the cabinet.

Marta's death was between Marta and me. I wouldn't allow Howard Dormin to direct the means.

He came up to the top floor a little while later, bearing a bowl of greens for the rabbits and a bowl of nuts for the squirrels. He seemed to take considerable delight in feeding these animals and called them all manner of pet names during the process. The rats remaining alive got nothing at all. "Makes them run around faster when you let them out," he explained. "I always kill the rats first."

I wondered aloud if the noise of Howard's shooting gallery didn't bother his grandfather downstairs.

Howard shook his head. "No sir," he said. "Not one bit."

The rats' blood, still damp on the floors, began to stink, and I had grown weary of examining the bullet holes in the plaster walls and the timbered roof.

Howard said, "I'll show you my room."

Gratefully, I followed him downstairs to the third floor. It was dark out now. The round window at the end of the hallway might as well have been shuttered and curtained for all the light that came through it.

"Don't your neighbors hear?" I asked.

"Hear what?"

"The shots upstairs," I said.

Howard paused with his hand on the knob of the door of his room. He looked at me and grinned. *"Nobody can't hear nothing,"* he said in emphatic triple negative. "Not with that pistol. No sir."

He turned the knob and opened the door. He flicked on the switch. Somewhat to my surprise, I found that the only light in the room was fixed on one wall no more than a couple of feet from the floor.

Howard ducked and proceeded into the room. I then saw why.

At head-height, all across the room, was strung clothesline, like the web of a deranged spider. And depending from what must have been hundreds of wooden clothespins were plastic bags containing Howard's belongings: his knives, his underwear, his scissors and picks, his kerchiefs, his socks, and his salves.

"Over here," said Howard, calling to me through the hanging forest of plastic-encased belongings.

I stooped and crept under, following his voice.

There was his bed: no more than two blankets and a pillow laid directly on the hard wooden floor. Howard sat cross-legged on the blankets and playfully slapped at a couple of the plastic bags that hung directly over his head. He pointed out a chair to me.

It was a regular carved oak chair, but the legs had been sawed off and now the seat rested directly on the floor. I arranged myself in it as comfortably as circumstance permitted.

"Did you like that pistol?" he asked with a leer. "Did you get off on it?"

His phrase repelled me.

"No," I replied, not certain why I told the truth.

Howard's face fell. "You don't like to shoot things? You don't like to make holes where there weren't holes before and stick pistols in holes that are already there and make them even bigger and blacker than they were formerly?"

"Sometimes," I equivocated. "But not today."

He waved it in the air before me.

Howard sighed and looked around. He peered up at the window behind him.

Just beyond the window was the brick face of an apartment building. It couldn't have been more than three or four feet distant. A portion of a lighted window was visible.

Howard yanked the cord of the only lighted lamp in the room from its socket. From that moment on we were lighted only by the illumination from that window in the building behind.

"Old lady lives there," said Howard, with disgust. "Red lips, red red lips and white powder on her cheeks. I show her my thing. I press it against the window. See?"

He slid his finger down a trail of white slime on the grimy glass of the single window of his room.

"She sees me," said Howard. "Opens her mouth and I want to stick something in it." From the pocket of his trousers he took a piece of metal. He pressed a kind of button on it, and a long thin sharp blade slid rapidly out of the end of it. He waved it in the air before me. "I want to nail her tongue to the table," he went on dreamily, raising his hand and lowering it, as if he held a hammer. "And mince it. *Mince it,*" he repeated happily, energetically performing that action with his very real knife against the floor. The attack left a precise cross-hatching. He slipped the blade back into its sheath and tossed it to me. It dropped with a clatter on the floor between us. I did not pick it up.

I watched the window for sign of the old woman and her red mouth, but that evening, perhaps, she had chosen not to appear.

Howard, after inveighing at considerable length against this neighbor, seemed to recover his purposeful conviviality. He no longer spoke of the pistol with which he had put paid to the five rats and the cardboard cutout. He ignored the knife that still lay on the floor between us.

He talked of his past.

He had been thrown out of high school for some misdemeanor. He wasn't specific as to its nature. I imagined it to be quite small, in fact, and it was the lightness of his crime that prompted his silence, not its magnitude or perversity. It pleased Howard to appear in the most lurid light possible, I felt.

He said, for instance, "This building, you know, around the corner, full of cows. Cows with these red mouths and long black throats, bleating at me out their window, calling, *Howard, Howard, come up and kiss me!*" He imitated the song of the old women in a high, wheedling, nasal voice. He seemed pleased with the effect and repeated it. He grinned: "Man gave me ten and said, *Do it.* So I did it."

"Did what?" I asked.

"Lit it. Torched it. Boiled it. Broiled it. Burned it down."

"For just ten?" I asked incredulously.

"It was what I wanted," he said quietly. His voice, his manner of speech, his very diction altered as he recalled: "I stood there. I watched. I said hello to the firemen. I heard the old cows' bleating. *Save me Howard save me Howard bring me medicine for my burns.* I saw them standing in their windows. *Save me Howard save me Howard.* I saw their hair catch fire and burn like matchstick flame."

He explained to me the best manner for torching a piece of residential property. He took from his pocket a key and held it up over his head so that it shone in the light from the next apartment. That key, he claimed, would open the basement door of any apartment building in the city. He pointed into a dim corner of his room, and I barely discerned there a large can with a metal pouring spout. It was filled with kerosene, Howard said, and poured over any pile of trash—as might be found in the basement of any apartment building in the city—would serve as ignition for a powerful conflagration.

He got up and left the room, carefully setting the skeleton key on the floor halfway between my chair and the canister of kerosene.

In Howard's absence I remained seated in the amputated chair. I left the key where it lay. I did not go near the can of kerosene.

When Howard returned, he saw the key still upon the floor, and in a moment of uncontrollable anger, he kicked it into the corner.

He had brought with him into the room a small alarm clock. He sat back down on his blankets and furiously wound the clock.

"Ten thousand doors into Hell," he murmured. "And they all swing both ways."

He set the clock on the floor between us. Its luminous face glowed faintly. It ticked away the seconds of our lives.

I had not yet been convinced, in my hour or so in Howard's company in this appointed place, that this was indeed Howard's house. It might merely have been a location, searched out, secured, and prepared for our meeting by Another who controlled Howard's actions and sought to control mine. Howard was a good shot, so much was undeniably true—rats cannot be taught to play dead and bleed on cue. But he might have trained elsewhere than on the shooting range at the top of the house. These plastic bags hanging from wooden clothespins on strung line in his room might contain his underwear and his small weapons, but they need not necessarily have hung there for long. I kept my eyes open for some incontestable sign that this was genuinely Howard's place of residence. In the room ostensibly his, I could find none.

I asked the location of the bathroom. Perhaps I would find something there, I conjectured, or on the way there or on the way back from there.

Howard described the path I should take.

I went out of Howard's room and down to the end of the hall. I quietly opened a couple of doors on the way, feigning confusion. Each of the rooms was a large square airy chamber, empty and dusty, eerily lighted by the proximity of fixtures in the apartments of the next building.

I went into the bathroom. I needn't turn on the light. Not more than a meter or so outside the bathroom was a red brick wall and the lower portion of someone's kitchen window. Even through the glass I could smell pungent Indian spices. On a counter I counted three pale melons. That kitchen lighted Howard's bathroom.

I did not relieve myself. I've total control over my bladder and my guts. Instead, I immediately opened the medicine cabinet. That, I told myself, would give some sort of evidence, though indicative of what I hadn't any idea.

The cabinet, an old-fashioned wooden sort set deep into the wall, was filled with bottles of medicine. I held up several in the light streaming in from the Indian kitchen. I glanced up sharply when a portion of a diaphanous spangled sari came between me and the light. When it went away again, I read on the prescription labels:

FOR THE USE OF
H DORMIN

or:

FOR THE USE OF
J DORMIN

I examined every bottle in the cabinet. Some of the labels were quite old and faded. Some of the liquids had congealed. Some of the powders had fused. Some of the solids had melted. The chest, as a whole, was such a miscellany and of such an antiquity that

I was propelled to the conclusion that the cacophony of bottles was ingenuous. That is to say, by reasonable extension, this was Howard's house.

I was, in some vague manner, disappointed.

I flushed the toilet, unbuttoned my trousers so that I might button them again insouciantly, and went out of the bathroom into the long dark hallway. I was suddenly aware of a kind of banging in the house. Howard, I supposed at first, must have gone back upstairs. He was slaughtering rabbits in an attempt to re-interest me in the efficacy of gunware.

Howard stuck his head out of the door of the room and peered down the hallway at me. I couldn't make out his expression in the dim light.

"That's Grandfather," said Howard.

The banging grew louder and somehow more raucous as it slipped out of rhythm with itself.

Howard came out into the hallway and closed and carefully locked the door of his room behind him. He led me downstairs to the hallway on the second floor. We picked our way by flashlight. The patterned runner on the floor was gnawed by rats. The banging became frenzied.

"He wants to get out," said Howard, uneasily shrugging. "The door's unlocked."

We went down to the end of the hallway and paused before a closed door that was like any other in the house but for a large rectangular slot that had been roughly hewn out of the bottom.

The banging abruptly ceased.

"The door is open," said Howard nervously. "Come out."

I heard a scrambling inside the room, claws on a bare floor.

Howard held the flashlight before him and pointed its beam toward the ceiling. On its way there, the light illumined his face and mine.

"It *used* to be locked," Howard explained. "But not any more. Now he doesn't really want to come out at all. He just likes to pretend that he's still locked in. Old men are fond of the fucking past."

I heard another scurrying within the room. Howard flipped the flashlight over and shone it down toward the rat-gnawn carpet.

There, thrust out of the hole at the bottom of the door, were two long thin scaled white arms, with gnarled fingers and discolored nails.

I retreated a step or two.

The hands and arms trembled, then were still, then in an almost casual way, they mimed the action of someone turning the pages of a book. I thought of a fragile, famous scholar, buried in the bowels of some great library, carefully leafing through an old and valuable volume, with a grace and a surety born of decades of careful scholarship.

Howard kicked at the scholar's hands, and they withdrew.

"Hand me a book," said Howard contemptuously and pointed behind me.

I turned around and noticed for the first time a small cabinet of books there. I poked my finger toward it, touched a book, ran my finger up the spine to the top of the sewn signatures, and tilted the book out toward me. I passed it to Howard.

He briefly shone the light over the spine. Fleetingly I saw the legend:

. . . OF
CIVILIZATION

J. DORMAN

"One of yours, Grandfather," said Howard with a sneer, dropped it to the floor, and kicked it through the hewn hole.

Behind the door, I heard the scrabbling again. I heard the book pushed across the floor. I heard the swish of drapery, and a pale yellow light was then visible within. I conjectured that Howard's grandfather had opened a curtain, so that he might read by the light from a neighboring building.

"My grandfather was born on the third of March, seventy-two years ago," said Howard in an unnatural, stentorian voice. "I was born on the third of March, twenty-two years ago. There is one of us every half century."

Howard's voice echoed in the dark hallway. He switched off the flashlight. When the echoes died down, I heard the turning of the pages of the book inside the room. The dim yellow light eked out of the hole in the door and seeped into the carpet beneath our feet.

I asked Howard why he had locked his grandfather in this room in the first place.

When Howard replied, he spoke in the stentorian, unnatural voice, and what he said was like a speech memorized:

"Grandfather began life as a truck driver, but they caught him running down small animals on purpose."

Howard paused; I heard a page turn within.

"He was a teacher, but they caught him beating all his girl students. He was a writer, but they caught him ripping pages out of library books. He was a postmaster, but they caught him spilling glasses of water into the stamp drawers. He was a police officer, but they caught him pissing against restaurant windows. Now he's paying for his sins."

Howard led me to the other end of the hallway. He leaned against the rotting banister. He looked up into the stairwell; he looked down into it; all was dark. He whispered to me: "I'm afraid of him. I'm taking out a contract on his life. I'm going to have him blown away. I'm going to have his brains torched."

"Why don't you do it yourself?" I asked curiously. "You have a gun," I pointed out. "You have a knife. You have a canister of kerosene, and I suppose you have a match."

"His door is unlocked," Howard whispered. His fear was genuine. "It hasn't been locked for years. Before I could squeeze the trigger, he'd tear my arm from its socket. Before I could take the knife out of my pocket, he'd crush my legs. Before I could spill the kerosene over him, he'd stick his fingers in my sockets and squeeze my eyes till they popped."

I lost all respect I'd ever had for Howard. He was craven. It was impossible, I saw now, that Howard was any sort of Messenger at all. He was not controlled by Another. It was doubtful he knew anything about Marta. His slime was putrid: he was not the father of Annie's brat. Guns and knives and canisters of kerosene cannot make up for a withered scrotum, and I despised Howard Dormin from the bottom of my soul.

I said to Howard: "It's time for me to go."

"Not yet," said Howard fearfully. He dragged me back up to his room. I stood outside the door as he unlocked it. I had no intention of going inside again.

I said: "I'm going down the hall."

I went into the bathroom again. From the medicine cabinet I took a large bottle of sleeping pills I had noticed there before. The date on them was recent. I put the bottle in my pocket.

I went back down the hallway. I glanced into Howard's room. He stood at the window, his trousers down around his ankles. He pressed himself against the glass. He screamed: "Look at it! Look at it!"

I went down the stairs. Howard's grandfather began banging again as I passed the second floor.

On the first floor, a vague sense of something left undone prevented me from leaving the house. I went into the living room. It was lighted by a streetlamp outside. I maneuvered my way around the furniture and the stacked boxes and approached the carved marble mantel. The gilded French clock ticked there. I peered at its face in the dim light. I struck a match and held it up before the clock. There, painted on the face, was the legend:

TEMPUS FUGIT

I placed the clock under my arm and walked out of the house.

14

The next thing I knew I was home. I placed the clock on my mantel. Its ticking filled the apartment.

In every room I heard the quarter-seconds scraping away. I stood in the darkened corridors, doors shut at either end, with my hands pressed against my ears, and the beating of the gilded French clock tripped in my coursing blood.

I went into my bedroom and against all custom, lowered the Venetian blinds. They were the old-fashioned sort, with wooden slats originally painted white, but I had scrubbed them clean so many times that all the paint had worn away, exposing the light-colored wood beneath. I excluded all light from the room.

I removed my clothes. I put on my blinders, with the white patch over my left eye and the black patch over my right. I burrowed down beneath the covers.

Behind my blinders, I could not see. No light came to me where I lay curled beneath the sheets, the blankets, and the spread. The room was wholly dark, and I was blinded.

The noise of the ticking clock at the other end of the apartment filled my brain and beat away there for the whole of the night.

It is only on Sunday that I sleep late. This particular Sunday I awakened toward noon and remained in bed, in my blinders, beneath the covers, with the blinds in the room drawn, for an hour longer. In the night, a pool of slime had seeped out of my body. It was a frigid pool about my loins.

I pushed back the covers, I pulled off my blinders. I rose from my sopping bed and raised the blinds.

The sky lowered. Wisps of cloud were torn apart by the upraised fingers of nearby chimneys and aerials. Drops of rain spattered my hand when I thrust it out.

I cleansed my body of slime and wrapped myself in a coarse black robe. I went into the living room, where the scraping of the gilded clock was neither louder nor softer than it had been in my bedroom all night long, and I stared for a little while at the bottle of pills I had set at one end of the mantel.

I emptied the pills into a pressed-glass candy dish, took the bottle into the kitchen, filled it with water to weight it, and then immersed it in a sinkful of steaming water.

I made coffee. I sat with my coffee at the dining room table, and in my carefullest chirography I penned the following brief note:

A True Friend
Respectfully Requests
That You Partake
Of the Enclosed

I returned to the kitchen and took the medicine bottle from the hot water. The gummed label bearing Howard's name and the direction of the pharmacy that provided the pills slipped off.

I washed away the remaining gum and carefully dried the container.

I took it to the living room and dried it once more. I placed the pills back inside the bottle one by one, counting them as I did so.

There were NINETY-FOUR.

The gilded clock ticked away the final moments of Marta's unhappy life.

I pitied her. So near her end and her release, and denied the comfort of that knowledge.

Contrary to my schedule, I arrayed myself in Suit S-4. That deviation was only a detail but it served to mark the importance of the day to me.

I left my apartment with the bottle of pills in my left hand pocket and the note in my right.

I walked directly from my building, Number FORTY-SEVEN, to Marta's, Number NINETY-FOUR.

I carried my black umbrella against the rain.

A lesser man might have worried that he did not know which apartment in the building was Marta's. I had every confidence that I would be shown the way. No such small point of ignorance would interfere with the careful scheme of my grand design.

My confidence in Fate was not misplaced.

I mounted the stoop of Number NINETY-FOUR with no idea of how I might gain entrance to the building or, once inside, how I might discover which apartment was Marta's.

Just inside the front door of the building was a young man dressed in a dark one-piece uniform, pressing a screwdriver against one of the postal boxes there. As I was taking down my umbrella, he looked up at me through the glass and smiled.

He was, I assumed, the building's Maintenance Man.

He also bore a startling resemblance to Howard Dormin. At first, indeed, I thought it *was* Howard, with the addition of a false moustache.

Further, I was almost certain that the moustache was false, for it appeared to have come unglued on the left side of his mouth, but then I saw that it simply did not exist there.

No one seeking to disguise himself, I reflected with relief, would employ but half a moustache.

The Maintenance Man of Number NINETY-FOUR was not Howard Dormin, therefore, and after a small hesitation, I returned his smile.

He stood up and opened the door for me. He motioned to me to come inside out of the rain.

"Are you the police?" he asked.

It was polite conversation. By no stretch of any diseased imagination do I resemble an officer of the law.

"Why do you ask?" I asked.

"Thought you might be wanting to ask questions about Mrs. Hodges."

I detected in his voice an uncanny resemblance to Howard's.

"Why would I want to do that?" I asked.

"She died in her bathtub. Her mother thinks it was murder," shrugged the Maintenance Man. "Maybe it was. I wasn't there."

"No," I said, "I don't know anything about Mrs. Hodges. I came to leave something off for a friend of mine, but I don't know which apartment she lives in."

"I can help you," said the Maintenance Man with a friendly smile. "Unless your friend was Mrs. Hodges. She's dead. Unless you're bringing flowers, of course."

"No," I said, "not Mrs. Hodges. A young woman called Marta. She's a waitress at the Baltyk Kitchen down at the end of this street. Do you know who I mean?"

I wanted, at all costs, to avoid having to provide a physical description. With my grand scheme so near to completion, I wasn't certain that I was up to that. And my aversion, though perfectly understandable, might yet suggest that my errand was sinister.

"Yes," said the Maintenance Man. "Number ONE-EIGHT. Next to Mrs. Hodges. It was Marta who found Mrs. Hodges."

I didn't know what I should do then. I was confident this friendly Maintenance Man would let me into the building, but I did not want to chance Marta's hearing me outside her door, opening it, seeing me there, questioning me regarding the pills I had left her, and so on and so on, till the whole tight perfection of the plan wound down in a welter of words and explanations.

"You're not her first guest," said the Maintenance Man in a low, insinuating tone.

"I beg your pardon," I said.

"Marta has lots of friends," said the Maintenance Man with a leering smile that might have been peeled right off Howard Dormin's face. "I've been in Marta's apartment lots of times."

"Oh yes?" I murmured, sickening at the very thought.

The Maintenance Man grinned. He had been polite to me at first, the way any good employee is polite to a guest of the establishment that employs him. But once I had mentioned Marta, his attitude had changed. We were comrades in his warped mind. He had taken a tone of repellant familiarity with me. "I was there last night," he grinned. "Fixing her leaky faucet. Unclogging her sink. Stopping her drip. Checking her plugs."

Despite the negative evidence of the half-moustache, I was very nearly convinced that it was Howard Dormin who stood leering before me.

"Marta the Waitress?" I asked, unable to excise the incredulity from my voice.

The Maintenance Man, who might or might not have been Howard Dormin got up in disguise, nodded with a knowing, conspiratorial smile.

"Number ONE-EIGHT," he repeated. He pushed open the inside door. "Go on inside. Knock loud just in case."

"Just in case what?" I asked.

"Just in case she's entertaining again, that's all."

The hallway of Marta's building was carpeted in a lozenge pattern, each white lozenge containing a black rose on a curved stem. The wallpaper was the negative image of this: a white rose on a curved stem set inside a black lozenge. I mounted the carpeted stairs.

Marta's flat was on the third floor, at the front. I took the note from my pocket and placed it on the floor underneath the door, with a corner of it protruding inside her flat. I placed the bottle of pills atop this.

For some time I stood silent and unmoving before that door, transfixed by the knowledge that she dwelled within. Marta—I told myself, and scarcely believing it, as an exorcist even as he pronounces anathema is never convinced of the reality of the devils that puff out the belly of the possessed boy—is behind

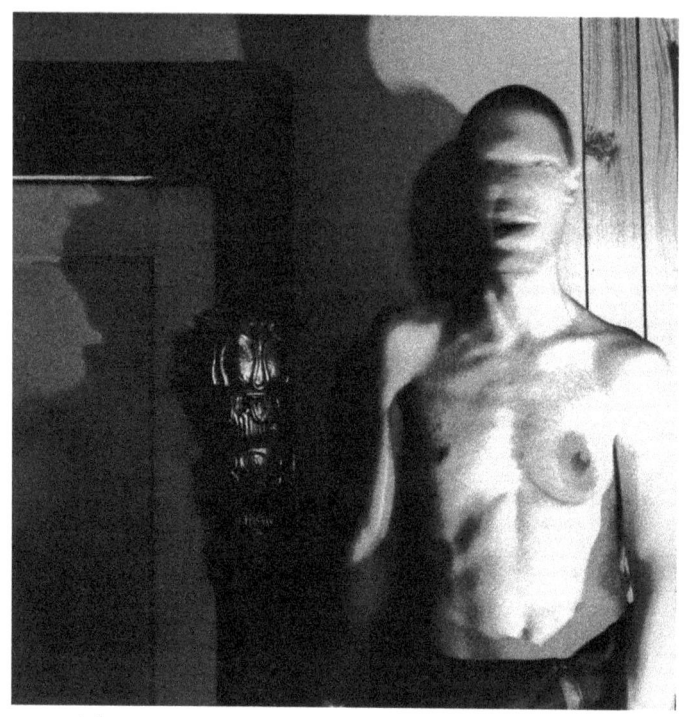

The Maintenance Man came forward into the light.

there. Her essence danced in the air that swirled through the keyhole.

I knelt and peered through, but for my trouble saw nothing but an expanse of bare painted floor.

I knocked loudly and rapidly three times and then fled down the stairs. I slowed only on the last flight. I did not wish to appear conspicuous.

When I reached the first floor, the Maintenance Man was gone. That was just as well. I was relieved not to have to explain to him why I had not stayed.

I put my hand to the knob of the door. I heard his voice behind me.

"She's in," he said. "I know she's in."

I turned around. The Maintenance Man stood in the shadows at the end of the hallway. He stepped forward toward me.

"I just wanted to leave her a little gift. A little surprise," I said. "So don't tell her who—"

I broke off in disgust.

The Maintenance Man had come forward into the light.

He had unzipped his uniform and the top half of it now fell about his waist. The arms of the uniform swung with a graceful languor as he moved.

The left side of his chest had hair, the same color as his partial moustaches. The right side was smooth but bore a fair-sized, fair-shaped female breast, with a large soft nipple spitting out from the center of it.

"If she's busy up there, come down to the cellar," he suggested. "Marta's all right," he said with lascivious deprecation, "but I've got variety..."

I turned and fled from the hermaphroditic abomination. *So much deformity beneath one roof* I thought, and was grateful I had seen no one else who lived in the building. On my reeling way out, I pressed the button for Number ONE-EIGHT. That was my only farewell to Marta. She was, I told myself, as good as dead.

15

Before I set out with the pills and the note, I had anticipated a homecoming shot through with a victorious glee. I would have provided Marta with the means to die. The Maintenance Man, however—a revolting example of the Third Sex, no less demanding of extinction than Marta herself, it seemed to me—had defiled all that.

Instead of an ecstasy of fulfillment, I felt only anxiety. I changed my suit. I still felt distraught. I took off my suit, put on a coarse white robe, and wandered room to room in my apartment. I sometimes lost myself in the corridors and found myself where I had not thought I would be.

I fretted.

I worried that Marta would not "do her duty."

She would find the pills, she would read the note, she would tear up the note, and broadcast the pills from her apartment window.

I had neglected to take into consideration that Marta was a flawed vessel. My perfect plan in my perfect mind had not made allowance for imperfection. Perhaps, after all, I should have taken Howard's advice: secreted a pistol and ammunition and gone that route. Pills befitted a subtle mind and a sensitive imagination. Pills might very well prove insufficient to the task.

I fretted too about the Maintenance Man in Marta's apartment building.

Away from there, I was no longer certain that he was not Howard Dormin after all. The single female breast was real enough, but that might always have been hidden beneath the loose shirts that Howard affected. In that case, the half-moustache might indeed have been faked. Certainly their voices were the same.

Supposing Howard was masquerading as the Maintenance Man: what did that mean?

Was he for me, or was he against me?

Was he there to make certain that Marta died, or that she lived?

And if the hermaphroditic Employee was not Howard, would he warn Marta against me? Or, supposing Marta died from the pills, would he alert the police to my presence and my appearance?

The possibilities, which branched out even further than this, were too vague and too numerous for me to puzzle through on a single rainy afternoon. I sat at the window that overlooked the street and watched for Marta's appearance on her way to work.

Marta did not appear.

Late that Sunday evening I went out to get something to eat. I passed the Baltyk Kitchen. For the first time since I had moved to that neighborhood, the restaurant was closed. I did not know why.

The next morning, which was still rainy, I sent my Employer the following message, by telegraph:

DEATH IN THE FAMILY

I knew he would realize who sent the message when I did not appear at the office.

That Monday was the first day I had taken off since I first went to work for my Employer.

The Baltyk Kitchen remained closed. I peered through the curtains. I could detect someone moving about inside.

I walked around all day long, carefully avoiding Number NINETY-FOUR. Several streets over, at the edge of my neighborhood, I came up half a block behind a young woman.

Even without the evidence of the striped trousers and the polka-dot blouse, I knew it was Annie. There is something characteristically gooselike in Annie's walk that becomes pronounced when she hurries.

I did not call out. I went forward, decreasing the distance between us. I determined to ask her what she knew about Marta. I'd be subtle, however. Sneaking, I'd bring the Baltyk Kitchen into the conversation and judge what effect the name had upon her.

Annie, to my astonishment, went up a broad flight of concrete steps and entered a church—The Church of All Souls. I wondered if, having sensed that I was following her, she sought to avoid me. I lingered a few minutes on the steps. The rain beat down all around me. Annie did not come out. I pulled open the heavy oaken doors and went inside.

In the vestibule I shook my umbrella dry. The rainwater splashed into the font of holy water.

I went into the sanctuary of the church and seated myself near the back in a dim unlighted corner. I heard the rain beating against the stained glass windows, barred against vandals. And beneath the rain I heard a confused murmuring from one of the confession boxes.

Presently, the curtain of the box opened and Annie crawled out. She hurried up the lateral aisle, tying a scarf around her head.

I slipped farther into the shadows. The pew whined beneath my trousers.

Annie genuflected before the altar and disappeared out the back of the church. For a few moments, as she opened the outer doors, I heard the rain more clearly.

I saw his heavy-lidded eyes staring back at me.

I rose and crossed the aisle, not genuflecting or even nodding or crossing myself before the altar. I pulled aside the curtain of the confessional Annie had left so hurriedly.

I heard the priest murmuring before I even entered the confession box. If he could begin without me, I could begin without him.

"Bless me, Father, for I have sinned," I whispered, as I pulled the curtain back into place. "It has been sixteen years since my last confession."

Alone together then, the priest and I fell silent at once.

The box was claustrophobic. Perhaps it was only that when I was last in one I was myself much smaller. There seemed to be no room for my legs. I had to fold my arms across my chest.

I peered at the priest through the grate. I saw his heavy-lidded eyes staring back at me.

The air was close in the confession box. It stank of schnapps and slime.

"Sixteen years," whispered the priest. He was drunk. He cast his bloodshot eyes over my face.

"Yes, Father," I replied. "But I came not to confess my sins but to proclaim the good that I have done."

"None of us is good," said the priest, slurring every one of the words.

"I am helping a young woman to die," I said. "I've given her sleeping pills and a note encouraging her to swallow them."

"That is a sin," said the priest, comfortably. "Three Hail Marys at the altar. Go and sin no more. The Lord be with you, and—"

"No," I said. "It is not a sin! She is Nature's blunder—an abomination before the eyes of the Lord. She apprehends this and desires sweet release! Marta—"

"We are all martyrs," said the priest, pressing his left hand against the grating. His ring finger was missing altogether, sheered off at the joint. The scar was recent.

I was silent a moment.

The priest began to sing, low and dismally, but with a strangely rollicking lilt:

By the light of burning martyrs,
Christ, thy bleeding feet we track . . .

"Not martyr," I said. "*Marta*. She accepts death. She has earned it. I'm her judgment, not her judge."

"Do you Flog the Bishop?" the priest demanded suddenly.

I didn't know what he meant.

"Do you Paddle the Pickle?" he went on impatiently. "Jerk the Gherkin? Bang the Banjo? Strangle the Stogie?"

I said nothing.

"Do you visit with Mother Thumb and her Four Children?" he cried in a hot whisper. "Play Solo upon a Private Pump Organ? Are you stigmatized with a Dishonorable Discharge?"

"This woman," I resumed. "Before the eye of God, she's—"

"*How often?*" demanded the priest excitedly.

"Once a day," I said.

There was a long pause. The priest breathed hard, harder, gurgled, groaned and sighed.

"That is a sin," said the priest in a strangled voice. "Five Hail Marys prostrate before the Altar."

He was as filthy as the gutters that wash away his vomit and his seed.

I returned home to wait. I passed the Baltyk Kitchen on the way; it was still closed. I spoke to a policeman on the corner. The policeman said, "They're on vacation, I heard."

A stranger, passing by at that moment and overhearing my question, differed. "No," he said, "I think there was a death in the family."

Scrawled on the door, in white chalk, was a winged hourglass.

Late into the night I sat at my living room window and watched the street. Once or twice I saw movement in the shadows on the opposite side, between parked vehicles and the brick houses there.

Late in the night, when the rain had left off and everything was still, I heard a woman's voice, calling up to me out of the darkness. She said: "No man knows the hour of his death."

Then I heard laughter, from all sides of the street, and the voices and the shadows melted away.

I stood up stiffly from my place at the window.

The gilded French clock on the mantel suddenly stopped ticking.

I was flooded with the certainty that Marta was dead.

16

I did not return to work on Tuesday. The day was warm. The previous evening's rainwater steamed off the streets. I was waiting for something but didn't know what.

I don't know now.

I grew slovenly. I did not cleanse myself, I ignored my schedule of suits, I wandered around my apartment either in my coarse white robe or else in my coarse black robe. My cleaning was neglected. I ate only when I was hungry, and then picked food directly out of boxes or spooned it directly out of cans or poured it directly from brown sacks into a single bowl that I rinsed over and over again. The slime built up in my testicles, and I made no effort to release it. I felt its slow poison seeping through my body.

I wasn't losing power, I knew that. I was only loosening a rope I had held taut for too long.

I wondered if all this didn't have something to do with Marta. Such a conclusion seemed plausible, since my malaise followed so directly upon my carrying out my plan to help her to die. Yet that decision had not been a mistake. I had never once doubted the propriety of my resolve. And subconsciously I did not feel guilt, either. I was very nearly certain of that. My thoughts were muddled. My logical apparatus had gone by the boards. I decided to starve myself to see if my thoughts and dreams would become clearer.

I put all the foodstuffs from my cabinets and my refrigerator into paper bags and carried them to the trash barrels in the basement. I wiped the shelves and counters free of crumbs. I burned incense in the kitchen to disguise the lingering odors of foods and dinners long past. I removed all the cookbooks from their twelve shelves in the corridor and stacked them neatly and in order, for purposes of easy reconstruction, on the kitchen floor. Then I nailed shut all the doors that led into the kitchen.

I sat in the living room and waited for the pains of hunger to assail me.

My thoughts remained muddled. My belly felt filled with food.

I watched at the window and could think of nothing but the fact that I wasn't eating, and that that appeared to make no difference to me.

I fell asleep on the sofa in the living room. In those few minutes my slime spewed out in the crevasse between the cushions.

When I awoke I tried to set the gilded French clock to ticking again. The mechanism required the turning of a key, but the key was missing. I did not remember having seen one at Howard's.

All my old patterns were smashed. I felt as if my life were falling apart.

I knew that I should think the whole matter through. My

intellect would put the pieces back together. But I couldn't even decide what I should think of first. I tried beginning at the beginning, at the sign that read:

DEATH IN THE FAMILY

Yet each time I began so, I was lost again before I even entered the Baltyk Kitchen for the first time.

I tried thinking of the persons involved, focusing on Howard or on Annie or on the hermaphroditic Maintenance Man of Number NINETY-FOUR. Yet each time I began so, my mind reverted to the inconclusive interview with the priest in the Church of All Souls.

I indulged this unlooked-for bent. I thought about this brief encounter.

I had not entered the confessional to obtain spiritual expiation for my crime. I had only followed Annie there. And once confronted with the priest, who did not know me and who was bound to keep my confession a secret, I had decided to tell him of my great project. I had wanted to indulge my pride—and that pride was perhaps my only sin. I did not trust Howard or Annie any longer, and for some time they have been the only persons I've been in the habit of speaking to at all. The priest was a mere convenience. Yet I suppose it was only right that he, ensconced in the confessional, should have imagined that I came to admit to some iniquity of conduct or thought. But if he had given me time, I feel sure I could have explained the whole matter to my satisfaction and his instruction.

Over and over again in my mind, I reviewed what he had said and what I had said, his tone of voice, my volume. I reconstructed the entire brief exchange. Over and over again, on an endless tape, I played it in my mind.

Why, I wondered, was the penance for masturbation greater than that for assisting a suicide?

The two voices sang in my mind. The priest's dialogue took on a rehearsed precision, his drunken accents sounded faked.

The accents of my own voice began to sound alien to me. There is nothing more contemptible in a man than a squeaking

The individual photographs were of Shade and Shadow.

voice. Listening over and over again to that interview, I began to detect a certain shrill, breaking quality in my own tones. I heard, as it were, an echo in everything I said. I heard first my voice as it sounded in my own ears: straightforward, masculine, pointed. Then a fraction of a second later, I seemed to hear the echo of my voice: strident, nasal, squeaking, the antithesis of all that a man's voice ought to be.

I took cash and went out and bought a tape recorder.

This required going to Annie's neighborhood, the nearest streets where such items may be got cheaply. Around there, for the benefit of the narrowly paid government workers, there are a number of narrow-front stores specializing in overstocks and markdowns. Their wares are spread out in a widening triangle of cartons and boxes and baskets, down the front steps and along the sidewalks, as if the building itself were regurgitating its inventory. Only persons interested in purchase walk that way since the route is so impeded with junk that a quick progress is impossible. I wandered for some little while among the agglomerations of dented, faulty, unusable merchandise until I at last discovered a small tape recorder. I took it inside and ascertained that it worked. I purchased several tapes as well.

I smiled as I came out the door again, for I had detected the first rumblings in my belly. Hunger showed that I was getting on the right track again.

I did not go directly home. Since I was in Annie's neighborhood, I decided to go by her store. I'd see if her belly had swelled.

Though ostensibly Annie and I had had no break in our relationship—I often left her apartment in the early morning without saying good-bye—my attitude toward her was changed. She was, in some vague but undeniable way, the enemy. I did not trust her. I did not know with whom she might be in league.

I went cautiously up to the storefront that housed her concern. I had no wish for her to see me before I was prepared to show myself.

I stood against a concrete pilaster just out of sight. From my vantage I could see quite clearly one of the machines in the front window and even make out the figures on the belt of photographs that was pulled wetly out of it.

The individual photographs were of Shade and Shadow, the twin female members of the Fuggits.

The two young women were naked, sitting together on a sofa with their legs spread wide. The pubic hair of one had been dyed jetty black, like her hair; the pubic hair of the other had been bleached very nearly white. The photograph disappeared back into the machine, to be dried and snipped off the roll.

But there were others, which I need not describe here.

I decided not to show myself to Annie, for obvious reasons.

I was making decisions. I was getting hungrier. Those were good signs.

I waited until a group of government office workers came up behind me on the sidewalk. Just as they were passing before the store, I joined their little group. Annie, if she looked up from her counter, would not notice me—she would see only a phalanx of workers such as pass her shop every day.

As I went by I glanced inside. There was Annie behind the counter. She wore a colored blouse, but my flawed eyes did not allow me to make out exactly what color.

Before the counter stood a man who turned in profile just as I passed.

I could not be surprised to find that it was Howard Dormin.

Or perhaps the Maintenance Man. My brief glance would not allow me to distinguish, if indeed, they were different persons at all.

I pressed the recorder and the tapes against the hollow of my stomach and turned into a street that would lead me back to my flat.

I did not take my normal route home from Annie's place. I did not know who might be lying in wait. Yet all the streets around there were tolerably familiar to me and I did not fear losing myself.

I congratulated myself on reaching home without untoward incident. However, just outside my own building, Number FORTY-SEVEN, I happened to notice an overturned food basket against a lamppost. It had evidently been stolen from some supermarket, though I didn't know of any in my immediate neighborhood.

As I was taking my latch key from my pocket, a woman approached me and touched my arm. She was small and dark, in her late thirties perhaps. I took her to be one of those gypsies who are habitually to be found in the parks of this part of the city, trying to sell artificial flowers "to help the children" or "to feed the hungry" or "to alleviate the mental suffering of the politically downtrodden," but really only to line their own pockets.

"Sir!" she called to me. "Do you have a piece of paper?"

"How large?" I asked warily.

"Small," she replied. "I want to let the supermarket know about their basket there in the middle of the street."

The woman spoke with a slight, indeterminate accent. I extracted a small sheet of paper from my pocket and handed it to her.

"Do you have a pen?" she asked. I handed her one.

"What is the name of this street, sir?"

"Hodges," I said and realized with misgiving that the gypsy had maneuvered herself so that she now stood between me and the steps up to the door of Number FORTY-SEVEN.

"Would you write that down please?"

I did so and stepped around her. I hurried up to the outer door of my building. I had the key in the lock when I was arrested by her imperative voice. "Sir! Sir!" She ran up the steps after me.

If I had been faster or more adroit with the latch key I would have fled inside, but she caught me there at the top of the steps. She handed me the scrap of paper on which I had written:

HODGES STREET

Unaccountably, the black ink had begun to run. The words were now almost illegible.

The woman asked me to write down the number of the building before which the overturned basket lay.

I pointed up at the number painted in large numerals above the door.

She shook her head uncomprehendingly. "Write it, please."

I wrote the number down and handed back the paper.

The woman smirked at me, whether in derision or simply thanks I couldn't make out, but she made no motion to move away.

I turned and placed myself between her and the door. I heard her shuffling uneasily behind me. I inserted the key and opened the lock. I slipped inside and went halfway up the first flight of stairs before I turned around and looked back. The gypsy had not moved. She glared at me through the glass panes. She rattled the knob of the locked door, trying to gain entrance. She beckoned me to open the door. I ignored her.

There was something vaguely sinister about this incident. By the time I reached the fourth floor, hugging my recorder and my tapes to my breast, I was no longer certain that the gypsy woman had nothing to do with Howard or Annie or the gang. I was convinced that she only wanted a specimen of my handwriting or something that belonged to me, that she might practice her sorcery on it. I discovered, when I had put down my burdens, that my pen was missing, too. She had somehow contrived to keep it.

My stomach rolled loudly with hunger, and I realized that I must keep up my guard.

I plugged in the tape recorder, unwrapped one of the blank tapes I had purchased, and set it inside the machine. I turned the machine on and took up the instruction book to read.

To my astonishment, the tape wasn't blank. A voice came on a few moments into the tape and said in a voice that sounded like my own in my head:

> Philosophy? I am a mysosophist! All
> wisdom is vanity, and I hate it!
> Autology is my study, autosophy my
> ambition, autonomy my pride. I am the
> great Panegoist, the would-be Conservator
> of Self, the inspired prophet of the
> Universal I. I—I—I! My creed has
> but one word, and that word but one
> letter, that letter represents Unity, and
> Unity is Strength! I am I, one,
> indivisible, central! O I! Hail and
> live for ever!

The rest of the tape was blank. When I played it over again, even that single speech—intoned in my mind's voice—was gone.

I recorded my own real voice into the machine. It came out another's. I repeated all that I had said to the priest. My words were strident, false, wheezing, and garbled. I wondered if I should have bought so inexpensive a machine. The fault might lie in the mechanism of the recorder. It might be in the tape. I switched tapes, I plugged in the recorder at a different outlet. The result was the same.

I recorded and re-recorded, and listened, and played back all day long. Soon the rumblings of my belly became loud on the tapes, louder than my squeaking voice.

I sounded like a ghost.

I desisted. The truth was not to be got out of machines. I took a knife and slit open the electrical cord, exposing the colored wires within. I took the tapes and ground them beneath my heel.

It was night, and I presumed, very late. The gilded clock on the mantel was no good to me. It had stopped at the hour of Marta's death.

I was no longer convinced, however, that Marta was dead. I think, had I alone been involved in this business, I would have rested secure in the thought of Marta's corpse, unmoving and unmourned, in apartment ONE-EIGHT of Number NINETY-FOUR. But here were Annie and Howard, the Fuggits, the hermaphroditic Maintenance Man, and even the spuriously drunken priest all concerning themselves with the death of this one, supremely hideous waitress.

Yet the fact was, I no longer cared. Whether Marta lived or was dead was a matter of indifference to me. I was only interested in getting my life in order again. I wondered, for instance, if I shouldn't return to work the following day.

I would, I decided.

This was a moment of great release to me.

I felt as if my life had suddenly dropped back into the security of my pocket once more.

It was late at night, but I dressed myself in Suit S-4 and went out. My own building was dark and still. The street was dark and empty. I walked up the street toward Number NINETY-FOUR. I was no longer afraid of it. I could gaze on its black windows with equanimity. Its smoke-drenched bricks held no terrors for me. The Maintenance Man might have lured someone into the basement and exposed his aberrant self, but I could stand without, on the sidewalk, and not care.

An ambulance was drawn up before the building. If its light had been flashing, I would have seen it sooner. The street was dark and deserted, the ambulance parked double in the street. I took up a position across the way and watched.

I heard a door open. I could just discern the figure of the Maintenance Man, pushing wide the outside door of the building. Two men in white uniforms emerged, bearing a stretcher between them. On the stretcher lay a sheet-covered body. They brought it down the steps and slid it unceremoniously into the back of the ambulance. As they climbed into the front of the vehicle, they called out thanks to the Maintenance Man. The ambulance pulled slowly away. The Maintenance Man went back inside. I continued to wait and watch. Two policemen came out of Number NINETY-FOUR a few minutes later. The Maintenance Man did not appear again.

For me time stopped, though around me the world continued to tick away. I was pressed against the brick wall of an abandoned house across the street from Number NINETY-FOUR. The light increased around me. The emptiness of my belly expanded until I seemed nothing but a shell of skin, held in shape only by Suit S-4. I did not breathe. I did not blink my eyes.

Now and then a vehicle passed. Now and then a rat hurled itself from one side of the street to the other. A man walking his dog passed me and glanced at me and glanced away.

I closed my eyes. At last I felt the emptiness that suffused my body working its way up into my head. My face and scalp were no more than the skin of a balloon.

I opened my eyes. I pressed my fingers against the clammy brick wall behind me and pushed away. Stiffly I walked to the curb. I paused for a moment, gathering strength and agility in my limbs—lighter now than if they had been thin rubber membranes stuffed with straw. I walked across the street and paused at the bottom of the stoop of Number NINETY-FOUR. I looked up at the door. I tried to tell myself that I wasn't fearful of the Maintenance Man and discovered that, in actuality, I had no fear left to overcome.

I went up the stoop. The front door was open. I went inside. I wondered which buzzer to push. I pushed Marta's.

Against all expectation, the lock on the inner door was released.

Not even thinking what this might portend, I stepped inside.

I went slowly up the stairs. I was weak with hunger. The staircase was unlighted. It was very soon after dawn. None of the residents of the house was stirring. I heard no noises behind the doors I passed. I felt the thick carpet beneath my feet and dragged my hand comfortingly along the banister. The door of ONE-EIGHT was wedged open.

I stood there and called inside, "Marta?"

It might, after all, have been someone other than Marta on the stretcher. A Mrs. Hodges had died just a few days before. Perhaps all the tenants were old, or perhaps they tended to be victims. Maybe one of them had stolen the pills I had left for Marta as well as the note. Perhaps it was Marta, expecting one of the many visitors the Maintenance Man claimed she entertained, who had wedged open her door. Perhaps she was herself inside, reclining on a sofa, with her peignoir pulled up above her waist. Perhaps, when I pushed open the door and stepped inside, the first thing I would see would be the gap between her thighs.

I pushed open the door and stepped inside.

On a sofa, with legs wide apart, sat the Maintenance Man with a leer.

"Is Marta here?" I asked.

"Marta went out," said the Maintenance Man.

I was no longer afraid of him. He stuck his hand into his shirt and began fondling his female breast. I looked around the room, and noted the furnishings.

Marta had rented her pieces from the same place I had got mine. I recalled this set of Mediterranean from the showroom. I wondered if she had paid for it in full before the place went out of business.

There were mirrors everywhere, at least two on every wall, some in gilt frames, some in silver frames, and some were merely squares of glass attached with adhesive. I could not but be surprised at this. Marta had not the sort of physiognomy that would do well so often reflected. But perhaps it would never have done to have forgot just what her appearance was. She could never risk being surprised by the horrible face of reality, thrown back at her by some chance reflection in a shop window or a still puddle.

"Look around," said the Maintenance Man.

I glanced at him curiously, wondering if, after all, he were Howard Dormin, with half a false moustache glued to his upper lip.

I couldn't decide anything but that it no longer mattered one way or the other.

I went into Marta's bedroom. Her bed consisted of five mattresses piled one on top of the other. A single sheet and a single blanket covered the top mattress. Two pillows lay on the floor. The sheet and the cases were stained with slime. I went into the bathroom. I opened the medicine cabinet but did not find the bottle of pills I had left at the door. However, I did find several bottles of medicine that had been obtained from the pharmacy that employed Howard. Somehow, I was not surprised by this coincidence.

I went back out into the living room. The Maintenance Man had removed his shirt. I looked carefully and this time without revulsion at his bi-partite chest. I refer to the Maintenance Man as *he* and *him* at the risk of accuracy; but I first saw him in a purely masculine guise and have been unable to think of him as otherwise since. The aureole of his female breast was wide and the nipple itself erect.

He was leafing through an album of photographs open on a low table before him.

"Marta's pictures are very interesting," he remarked. "Do you want to see?"

I went over and glanced at the open album. I turned a couple of pages and looked at a few more of the grainy, black-and-white prints.

"They don't interest me," I said. "I've seen them before."

"Are you sure?" said the Maintenance Man, insidiously. He turned the album page and pointed to a particular print. It was grainy and blurred, but the woman in it was unmistakably Marta.

The man standing beside her was my brother, whose taxi wrecked just outside the Baltyk Kitchen.

The Maintenance Man turned the page.

There was a large print of the Fuggits, standing in a crescent at the top of the stoop of an apartment building. Marta herself stood only a step or two below them. She held up an imaginary camera to her face, pretending to photograph the photographer. The number over the door was FORTY-SEVEN. Marta and the Fuggits were standing on the stoop of my own building.

I grew ill.

The Maintenance Man turned the page.

Here was Annie, on a bed, her naked belly crossed by the shadow of the photographer. In a mirror behind the bed was reflected the photographer's face. It was blurred and dim, and I couldn't quite make it out.

"Is this you taking the photograph of Annie?" I asked, unsure. "Or is it my friend Howard Dormin?"

"Photographs have no warmth," said the Maintenance Man as he stood up and began to unbutton his trousers.

"Will Marta be back?" I asked.

"Doubtful," replied the Maintenance Man. "But it don't matter. I'm here. I'll do, no matter what your taste is."

I turned away, just as he was lowering his pants.

"I'm half of this," he said quietly, "and half of that. I'm part Indian and part Negro. My father was a northern Protestant, my Mother a southern Catholic. I'm dark on the left and fair on the right. I'm generally on top but for the right person I don't mind sliding underneath."

I pulled the door of Marta's apartment slowly shut behind me.

Hunger had passed me. I no longer even desired food. My belly was quiet.

I went down the stairs and out the front doors of Number NINETY-FOUR. The morning was advancing. The light was brighter.

I walked toward home.

17

As I walked toward home I considered the question: *Is Marta dead or alive?*

I had no real evidence either way. I had seen someone's corpse taken from Number NINETY-FOUR, but there was no name emblazoned upon the sheet to tell me whose it was. The ambulance attendants did not announce the corpse's identity as they came down the steps bearing the stretcher between them.

Upstairs in Number NINETY-FOUR, the Maintenance Man had said only that Marta had gone away and that it was doubtful whether she would soon return. Such an assertion would be appropriate either for Marta's death or her going to the shore for a few weeks' vacation.

I had not found the empty pill bottle in Marta's flat, but this did not materially argue for her survival. Either the ambulance attendants or the police might easily have taken it away.

I did not go to work after all. I stayed in my apartment. I took the gilded French clock from the mantel and placed it on the dining room table. I pried off the back and took apart the mechanism bit by bit, laying the innards out in orderly rows until the entire table showed rank upon serried rank of gears and springs and cogged wheels.

I was buoyed, as I worked on the clock, by a feeling of freedom and contentment I had not enjoyed in a great while. I wondered whether this sense of completion, of union with myself, was not predicated upon an unconscious assumption that Marta indeed was dead. Would I be so happy, I wondered, if I happened to glance out my living room window and see Marta passing on the walk below, on her way to work at the Baltyk Kitchen?

I went to the window and looked out. It was nearly dusk, and the sky was darkening in the east. I saw my neighbors on their way home from work. Someone was moving out or moving in, a few doors up the street, and the moving van was blocking traffic. Vehicles were lined up behind it to the next intersection, blowing their horns obstreperously. I did not see Marta. My good feelings persisted.

I stood at the dining room table and admired my handiwork. I would not, for the present, put the clock together again. I wanted to savor its disembowelled state. When it got too dark to see the toothed wheels and the springs, I put some money into my pockets and went out in search of evidence that Marta was really dead.

I went to the corner. The Baltyk Kitchen was still closed. Someone had washed off the chalked winged hourglass on the door. Around the corner I stopped at a newsstand and began picking out several of the city and neighborhood papers, even those printed in foreign languages I did not read. Standing next to me was a bundled-up little girl, who, I realized in a moment, was not a little girl at all but a very small old woman. She picked up a copy of a popular general interest magazine from the top of a stack, held it up to the light of the streetlamp, and suddenly shouted: "What the hell is it with these wrinkles?" She threw the periodical onto the sidewalk. She picked up another, whose cover had also been creased slightly. "Why do I always get dumped on?" she protested loudly to me and overturned the whole pile, trying to find one, on the very bottom, that was unblemished.

I reached forward with two bills, to purchase the newspapers I had selected, and inadvertently I suppose I trod upon the old woman's foot.

"Your leg!" she screamed and overturned another stack of magazines in her distress. "I know why you put it there! Take your foot off mine! You send them to school and they come back stupider than when you sent them. I'll cut it off," she threatened, but I did not attend to her. The proprietor of the newsstand hurried around and drove her away, execrating her for spoiling his merchandise.

I entered a small cafe. As I went through each of the papers carefully, I broke my fast with a bowl of soup and, a little later, a plate of chopped rare steak.

I found nothing in any of the three city dailies. I went even more carefully through the two weekly papers that are printed for the benefit of this and some of the adjacent neighborhoods.

I ordered coffee and a pastry and then began to peruse the foreign language papers.

In the third of these, printed in the Cyrillic alphabet, I came across a brief article, in a wide black border, which several times repeated the name:

MARTA ALEKSANDROVNA BLYUSHKINA

This I took to be notice of Marta's death, though—when it came down to its being written in a language I didn't know and in an alphabet I wasn't familiar with—I couldn't be absolutely certain.

I tore out the page that contained the black-bordered tribute to the dead waitress, put it into my pocket, and left the cafe.

The name of the cafe was *Time and Tide*, but I noticed that only as I left it.

The evening was warm. Many old people were seated on their stoops, talking to one another and to their neighbors who passed on the sidewalk. Children played in the darkened street, and stumbled often, and cried loudly when they were hurt. I walked home slowly, wondering if I would ever know for certain if Marta was dead or not.

I walked past Number NINETY-FOUR. Only one apartment was lighted, and that was Marta's. Someone stood at the window and looked out. I glanced only to make certain it wasn't the waitress. It obviously wasn't, but the figure looked familiar. I did not, however, pause to study it. When I had walked past, I realized that the figure had resembled no one more than Annie. I retraced my steps, but when I got back to Number NINETY-FOUR, the figure in the window was gone and the lights in the apartment had been extinguished.

I was still thinking of Annie when I entered the vestibule of my apartment building, Number FORTY-SEVEN. Just inside the door were Shade and Shadow, Clay, Ashes, and Dust. Shade and Shadow smiled at me and took my arms. I could not tell the men apart, but one of them kicked me in the belly. I bent forward double and howled with the pain. The second of them pressed the back of his forearm against my brow to hold down my head; with his other hand he grabbed a handful of my hair and pulled and twisted until he had torn it out by the roots. He let me go; my scalp felt as if it were on fire. He had exposed the four wounds made by the terns nine years previous. Shade and Shadow still held me upright by my arms. I looked up. The third one took out a knife—exactly like the knife Howard showed me in his room—and released the blade.

I thought he would come at me, but he remained still.

Shade and Shadow pushed me toward him.

He raised the knife above my head and brought it down on the newly denuded spot on my scalp. He pressed it in, and though I felt the pressure, I felt no additional pain. He slowly drew the point of the knife down the side of my head, parting the hair and the skin beneath, just behind my ear, down along the side of my neck. Then, turning his wrist, he slipped the edge of the knife neatly beneath the collar of my shirt and pushed it along the line of my shoulder. He withdrew the knife and wiped the bloody blade on the sleeve of my jacket. Then he pressed the point of the knife slowly through the lapel of my suit jacket. Eventually I felt the point of it against the skin of my shoulder. I felt it pierce the skin. I felt the blood flow over my breast inside my shirt.

"Dust," I said, guessing.

He nodded.

Dust brought the blade of the knife down slowly, not as if he was deliberately cutting, but rather as if the handle were simply too heavy for him and he were allowing it to fall of its own weight. It cut through my suit jacket, my shirt, my undershirt, my skin, and the muscles of my chest.

He cut all the way down from my shoulder to my ankle.

My trousers and belt were sliced through and would have fallen off me had not Shade and Shadow pressed my elbows against my waist to hold them in place.

Dust knelt before me and sliced open my shoe from tongue to toe. My black cotton sock inside sagged apart. The sole of the shoe filled with the blood from my lacerated foot.

I did not doubt this action was to be repeated on the right side of my body.

It was not. Dust wiped the blade of his knife on the cuff of my split trousers, replaced it in its sheath and slipped it into his pocket again. Ashes and Clay had already left. Shade and Shadow pushed me forward and I fell against the stairs. By the time I had raised myself, they all were gone.

For the first time since I had come to live in Number FORTY-SEVEN, I took the elevator up. I leaned against the wall inside for support. When the elevator came to rest at my floor and I pulled away, I found that I had left a long narrow line of blood there, from the height of my head all the way down to the tiled floor of the elevator.

The elevator door opened but I did not get out. I remained behind the cast-iron grating, staring at this narrow line of blood. I stared, because something extraordinary had occurred.

The blood was red.

It was a deep crimson, very near a vermilion.

Even in the dim light provided by the low-watt yellow bulb embedded in the ceiling of the elevator, the color of my blood pulsated in its intensity.

I had experienced no such perception of color since the day, the hour, the very minute I was attacked by the terns in their nesting ground.

In nine years I had seen no color such as the color of my blood upon the wall of the elevator.

I peered up at the yellow light to see if it, too, were different.

The bulb was the color of dense morning urine, but it shone.

I leaned against the walls of the elevator and peered at them. I could make out flecks of bright purple, bright blue, bright orange, mere stains and chips and idle brushings, but they were magical in my long-deprived eyes.

I dreaded leaving the elevator. What if the ability to appreciate these intensities of colors was confined to this small space? What if outside it, I returned to my drab perception of grays and whites and blacks?

That was, however, nonsense. It could not be so. I had just been beaten, and that beating restored to its proper sphere whatever it was the attack of the terns had knocked ajar in my head. My sight was repaired. I wondered how my apartment would appear to my new eyes.

Trembling, I pushed aside the grating. I stepped outside into the hallway and withdrew my key from my pocket. This was a delicate operation, since with one hand I must hold up my trousers, which were in every danger of tumbling down around my feet. And I limped for the injury done my foot. I still bled. But what mattered these things when the farther reaches of my sight had been restored to me?

I blessed the winged hourglass in my soul.

The elevator grate sprang shut. The mechanism of the elevator was roused into action by some other tenant on some other floor. It began to descend with a loud grating whirr.

In that same instant, the bright color that had flooded my brain began to fade.

I cried out, "No!" and threw my hands over my eyes.

I fell forward onto the floor, weeping. I crawled toward the door of my flat, leaving my shredded trousers and a trail of blood behind.

I pulled myself up along the doorjamb. The knob of the door and the keyhole beneath it were blurs behind a web of darkness that was growing thicker in every strand over my accursed eyes.

Not only my perception of color, but my very sight itself failed as I inched upward.

By the time I got the keys into the locks and had pushed open the door and stumbled headlong into the first narrow corridor of my flat, I was wholly blind.

I sat for a long while with my back against the door, wondering what to do. I may have slept, for at some point I seemed to rouse myself.

I rose, pushing myself up along the plane of the door. Unthinkingly and out of sighted habit, I spun the combination lock that was on the inside.

I now was locked inside the apartment. I had no way of getting out for I could not see the numbers on the lock. I had no telephone with which to call for assistance, and had I had a telephone, there would have been no one to call. It was no comfort to think that if worse came to worst—and it already *had*, I considered ruefully—I might beat upon the walls and summon my neighbors. For my nearest neighbors were madmen. I might call out of my windows, but I was certain that some member of the gang would be on watch, and it would be Shade or Shadow, Clay, Ashes, or Dust alone who came to my assistance.

I resisted an impulse to panic. I felt my way to the bathroom, removed my clothing, and climbed into the bathtub. The stinging nettles of the shower water would have been exquisite torture on my long threadlike wound.

I lay beneath the warm water and shook my body slightly. The seeping blood from my wound swirled away into the bath—I could taste and smell it in the water.

I let the water flow out of the tub. I filled it again. I carefully soaped the wound and probed every inch of the narrow trench made by Dust's knife. I pressed my fingers in that tender furrow between the hedges of flesh that had been raised on either side. It seemed, at least, no longer to bleed.

I rose from the bath and went to the medicine cabinet. I fumbled among the bottles there until I found one that was square and the correct size as I remembered it. I removed the top and sniffed it—there was no mistaking the stink of merthiolate. Holding the closed bottle tightly in one fist, I felt my way to the living room. I lay down upon the sofa, still naked, and propped the bottle on my chest. I unscrewed the cap and methodically brushed the stinging liquid into the wound, beginning at the top of my head and proceeding all the way down to my foot.

I flinched and hissed through my teeth at the pain.

Dust had done a careful job, I had found, and had connected the three separate incisions into a single long line, from the crown of my head to the extremity of my left foot.

When I was done, I lay still from the exhaustion brought about by so much tension in my bracing against the pain.

I slept I think, just as I lay. When I woke, the long wound along my body throbbed even more loudly than before, but I felt that I now had it under my control.

I was hungry, but the kitchen was sealed and empty anyway. I could not get out the front door, and the back door—even if I could have got to it—was nailed shut. And even had I reached the street, how would I, so recently blind, have maneuvered myself?

I wandered the flat naked, wondering how I should occupy my time.

I wondered, in fact, how much time I had left to occupy.

I thought about resuming my regimen of cleaning, but this I found, after only a few moments of selecting the proper cloths by touch, hadn't its former charms.

I ended up sitting at the dining room table. I began putting the gilded French clock back together again.

This was necessarily a slow operation, as I was blind and must not only remember, in reverse sequence, exactly how the thing was taken apart, but must find the pieces by touch. To translate a visual memory into a tactile contemporaneity is a tricky task. Yet by dint of patience and a refusal to consider the helplessness of my lot, I proceeded.

The hours passed. So much I could tell by the faint chiming of a church bell in the distance. I had never, in my sighted days, heard it. I could tell when the night had ended and the morning begun by the increase in temperature inside the apartment and the rise in traffic on the street outside.

As I worked with the clock, I considered my present predicament. I analyzed not so much my feelings, as what I felt. At the same time that I felt completely empty, empty of all desire and all regret, I felt infused with an intense and searching calmness, like a philosopher, all alone, who thinks in search of a thought.

I wondered, as I walked naked about the dining room table, pressing my thumbs against each of the springs, gears, and cogs in their serried ranks in search of the next and only correct piece, if I actually even existed. It occurred to me, in my blindness, that all along, it had not been the vindication of my perfection but rather the mere destruction of Marta that had been of paramount importance to the world.

That is to say, the justification for my birth, my decades of upbringing, education, housing, and sustenance, had been that one day I would conceive a plan to do away with

MARTA ALEKSANDROVNA BLYUSHKINA

It was she, therefore, who had been of real significance. I didn't understand this, I wasn't certain I believed it, but I had to admit the possibility of its validity. In any case, if it were so, then once Marta was dead, my duty—my very *raison d'être*—was finished. There was no longer any justification for my existence.

And perhaps I did not, after all, exist. Perhaps I lay dead in the lobby downstairs, my corpse awaiting discovery. An oily black smudge on the plaster wall there marked the egress of my soul.

These tactile sensations were merely the occult residue of my very nearly indomitable being. They would fade as I continued my delicate work, and the clock never be whole again.

These and other such thoughts occupied me at the dining room table. The ranks of the parts of the clock's mechanism became depleted. The hours were counted off by the distant church chimes. That day faded into night again.

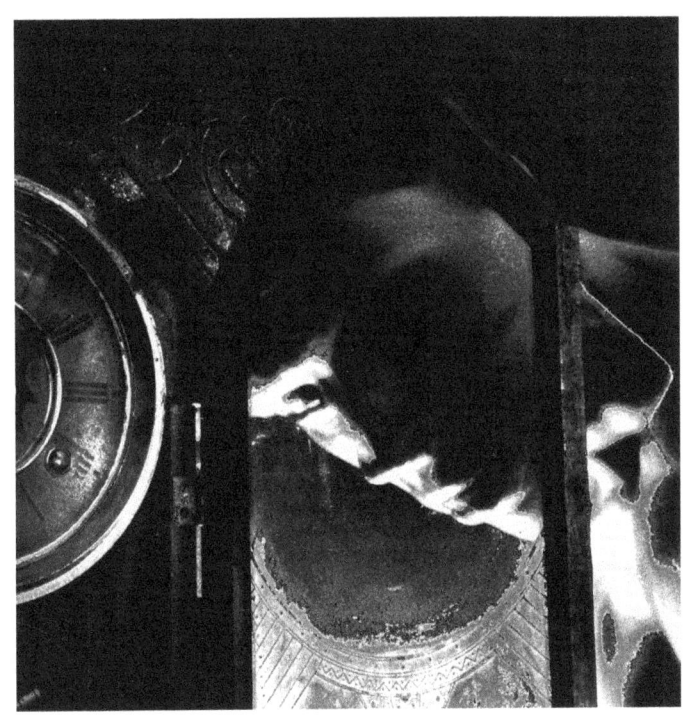

It was late at night when I finished the clock.

I no longer fretted.

It did not matter that I had not eaten in much more than twenty-four hours, that possibly my wounds were infected, that —as I had not had a visitor in more than three years—it was unlikely anyone would chance by now to rescue me in my helpless condition. It was no longer even of any concern to me whether I existed or not.

When it came down to it, my only thought was for the clock.

When I ran my thumb over its face, I could make out the raised Roman numerals and the legend:

TEMPUS FUGIT

It was late in the night when I finished the clock. I had been blind, I calculated, twenty-seven hours. I am, of course, twenty-seven, but the congruence didn't seem of overwhelming significance. In those twenty-seven hours, I had neither eaten, nor drunk, nor relieved myself. It was possible I had slept or dreamed, but I could not remember with any certainty.

I walked from the dining room table to the mantel and back again, memorizing the path. Then I took up the clock carefully and carried it to the mantel. I set it in its place.

Sighing I sat down on the couch and turned my head that way. My sightless eyes gazed with rapture at the restored clock.

I wondered what I should do next.

Nothing else in the apartment wanted repair.

On an impulse I rose and went to the front door. I decided to play with the combination lock just to see if I could open it by some sixth sense.

It is set, as I have mentioned, at 1/3/12, the month/day/hour of my birth.

I turned the lock once, twice, thrice.

It slipped apart in my hand.

At that same moment, the gilded clock on the mantel resumed its ticking.

Before I had even time to grasp this small, doubled miracle, the clock was chiming the twenty-seventh hour of my sightlessness.

I wept, and as I wept the miracle turned tri-partite.

My tears washed away my blindness.

Not only was my sight restored, but I was no longer deprived of color.

I saw that, in reality, the walls of the hallway were a dim green. I exalted in the subtlety of that green. The carpet was a faded gold. I rejoiced that I could gauge such a diminution of intensity. I gazed down at my naked, trembling body. The wound along the left side of my body was a pale livid red. The broken flesh was a mottled pink. My unscarred nipple was a creamy brown, the hairs around it were lightly tinged with yellow.

Marta was dead, and Marta—I understood now—had paid the price of my redemption.

I blessed her all unconscious in my heart.

The clock continued to tick upon the mantel.

I shut the door to the hallway and turned back to my apartment. I rushed room to room, gazing at everything with my new eyes. Every object, every inch of wall and floor and ceiling was different and new to me for its acquisition of color. Even the very air was suffused with dye.

I came back to the clock at last. I stared at its gleaming gilded case, understanding for the first time why mankind lusted so after gold.

I raised my eyes in ecstasy—and realized that my self-portrait was missing.

In its place, chalked on the patterned paper there, was a large winged hourglass and beneath the hourglass, the legend

TEMPUS FUGIT

I was no longer afraid. The gang had only been a part of my redemption. The wound that had opened up the left side of my body had been necessary to my restoration.

I went into the bathroom and looked at myself in the mirror.

If the self-portrait was missing, perhaps I, too, was no longer there.

I wasn't gone. I looked back at myself out of the glass.

My ordeal had left me haggard. The wound along the left side of my head throbbed with the pulse of my heart.

I gazed at myself for a long while.

I said to myself aloud:

What's next?

AUTHOR'S NOTE

This work of fiction is not a true story. The episodes, though perhaps in some cases based on fact, have been altered beyond the recognition of even those individuals intimately involved in the original incidents. The behavior of the terns in Chapter 2 is, however, consistent with the most recent, though yet unpublished, studies of the nesting habits of shore birds.

Also, it has recently come to my attention that there are at least three other writers publishing under the name Michael McDowell. I would like to make it clear that I am none of them.

MMM
Thanksgiving
Mystic Street

MICHAEL MCDOWELL was born in 1950 in Enterprise, Alabama and attended public schools in southern Alabama until 1968. He graduated with a bachelor's degree and a master's degree in English from Harvard, and in 1978 he was awarded his Ph.D. in English and American Literature from Brandeis.

His seventh novel written and first to be sold, *The Amulet*, was published in 1979 and would be followed by over thirty additional volumes of fiction written under his own name or the pseudonyms Nathan Aldyne, Axel Young, Mike McCray, and Preston MacAdam. His notable works include the Southern Gothic horror novels *Cold Moon Over Babylon* (1980) and *The Elementals* (1981), the serial novel *Blackwater* (1983), which was first published in a series of six paperback volumes, and the trilogy of "Jack & Susan" books.

By 1985 McDowell was writing screenplays for television, including episodes for a number of anthology series such as *Tales from the Darkside*, *Amazing Stories*, *Tales from the Crypt*, and *Alfred Hitchcock Presents*. He went on to write the screenplays for Tim Burton's *Beetlejuice* (1988) and *The Nightmare Before Christmas* (1993), as well as the script for *Thinner* (1996). McDowell died in 1999 from AIDS-related illness. Tabitha King, wife of author Stephen King, completed an unfinished McDowell novel, *Candles Burning*, which was published in 2006.*

HARRY O. MORRIS lives in New Mexico. He works in the basement and seldom leaves the house. He also has many mannequins.

---

* Michael McDowell's bio in the original printings of *Toplin* read: "Michael McDowell lives in Massachusetts. He writes in the mornings and spends the rest of the day looking out the window in hope that something interesting will happen. He collects photographs of corpses."